T0194968

BEST
EROTIC ROMANCE
2014

BEST
EROTIC
ROMANCE
2014

Edited by
KRISTINA WRIGHT

Foreword by
LAUREN DANE

CLEIS
PRESS

Published in the United States by Cleis Press, Inc.,
221 River Street, 9th Floor, Hoboken, NJ 07030

Printed in the United States.
Cover design: Scott Idleman/Blink
Cover photograph: Juhasz Peter/Getty Images
Text design: Frank Wiedemann

First Edition.
10 9 8 7 6 5 4 3 2 1

Trade paper ISBN: 978-1-62778-009-4
E-book ISBN: 978-1-62778-022-3

CONTENTS

FOREWORD

I write *those books*.

So often we see things that are created overwhelmingly by women mainly for the enjoyment of women—especially those things that tell women their sexuality is beautiful and absolutely okay—referred to in insulting and patronizing terms. As if by being mothers we are sexless robots only suited for ferrying children from place to place and folding laundry. As if being a wife or a partner means we're incapable of that slice of desire and heat when we catch their scent in the bathroom after they've left for work, or when we daydream at the office. As if we simply do not exist as sensual, sexual beings because as women we are not allowed to be or we risk being mocked and ridiculed.

We end up in a cultural catch-22 where if we are sexual we're nymphos, and if we are not sexual we're frigid. We cannot win in the world created by those who coin terms like *mommy porn* because those terms are laden with fear at the very idea that women are capable of being more than one thing, that we enjoy having sex more than folding laundry.

Which is why I think erotic romance is wonderful and revolutionary in the best sorts of ways.

I write *those books*—meaning erotic romance—because I love to write about connection. Because I believe women are worthy of stories where their strength and sexuality are described in positive terms. Because being in love and being connected to a partner is wonderful. I believe the heart of any real story worth telling or reading is about the connection of the people on the page. Be it thrillers, science fiction, romance, whatever.

To me, there is nothing more wholly female positive than a story where a woman opens herself up to the delights and annoyances of entering into a sexual and emotional relationship with a partner. I love to write about (and read about) emotion and yes, I love to write about sex and women who are smart and in the driver's seat when it comes to their sexual agency.

Erotic romance throws open the bedroom doors absolutely, but that's not the only hallmark of the genre. Erotic romance delves deeply into the physical and emotional connection between the people on the page and how their relationship progresses. Sex is a huge part of that and when it's done right, sex is the map of their romance.

I often hear people say things like, "You could just take out the sex and the story would still be great," and I think, "Oh, but who wants that?" I want to read a story where every bit of the potential is used. I want that bedroom door open and I want to see into the hearts and minds of the characters on the page. I want to be along with them on their journey to their Happily Ever After.

In this anthology you'll find sixteen stories of sex and love between all sorts of people. Because all sorts of people deserve sex and love. Playful, dark, fun, serious, rough and fast, slow and intense. It can be gentle, a breath of a kiss against a shoulder blade. Sometimes it's about finding your way back after being a bit lost, or the brand-new spark as you first meet. It's all hot. It's all sexy and emotional and it's all about connection.

Enjoy *Best Erotic Romance 2014* in all her guises—I know I did. And remember what E. M. Forster said in *Howards End:* "Only connect the prose and the passion, and both will be exalted, and human love will be seen at its height."

Lauren Dane

INTRODUCTION:
A PERFECT COMBINATION

Love and lust, that's what I need—what I *crave*. Love and lust: they belong together. Like peanut butter and jelly, like strawberries and champagne, like cookies and milk. Love and lust just *go* together. And while one is certainly fine, wonderful even, the combination is...incendiary. It's the magic combination of elements, with the planets aligned just so, that poets and songwriters have long attempted to capture in rhyme and meter. But it is erotic romance authors who invite us into that world of desire and longing, capturing those relationships that are so powerful they defy all odds.

This is the third edition of the *Best Erotic Romance* series and I believe I have selected stories that perfectly capture the combination of love and lust. Whether it's new lovers, as in Annabeth Leong's "Professional, Knowledgeable and Very Thorough," or familiar lovers such as the married couple in Victoria Blisse's "A Competitive Marriage," the passion is palpable on the page. Nikki Magennis writes about lovers who are also parents in "The Shortest Day," two people scraping by with so little alone time it feels as if their desire for each other will never be quenched. But they find a way. They *always* will.

Those who love and lust for each other will find a way, whatever it takes. And that's the theme of *Best Erotic Romance 2014*—lovers in love finding a way to be together no matter what the odds. It's idealistic, but not unrealistic. If you've ever known that kind of heart-pounding love and toe-curling desire, you know you'd be willing to do almost anything to hang on to it. And why shouldn't you? That kind of magic doesn't come along very often and when it does, when it's so right that even people on the street comment on how happy you are together, it's worth fighting for. The cynics will scoff and say it doesn't exist, the kind of passionate love found in these stories, but the authors represented here are romantics, not cynics. They believe in love—erotic, intimate, *connected* love—and so do I.

As I sit here in my usual corner at Starbucks drinking my iced coffee and writing about love and sex and what it all means, two texts just came up on my phone. They're from my husband. The first one says: *We need bread for dinner. Could you get some on the way home?* The second one says: *Smile! I love you, sexy.* Twenty-three years of marriage and he still loves *and* desires me—and the best part of it is, it's mutual! I believe in what I write because I live it. I hope you have the love and passion you want in your life—if not now, then soon—and I hope once it arrives you will hang on to it and never let go.

Whatever it takes, right? That's what we need.

Kristina Wright
In love in Virginia

THE SHORTEST DAY

Nikki Magennis

The alarm went off like a robotic bird chirping.

"No," Lucy said, slapping at John's arm, "please don't let it be morning."

A dim gloom was turning the curtains semitransparent. In a few hours, the light would be failing again. She rolled over and curled into John to breathe in his warm, familiar smell. But he was already swinging his legs out and staggering to the door.

Five minutes later, when he came back in still wet from the shower and threw a towel at the pile on the floor, the shock of his nakedness made a light flare in her. Then the kitchen broke out with bleats that the cereal box was full of milk and someone screamed and she blinked and John was gone, tugging on jeans and grabbing for a shirt, his wet blond hair still dark with water, sticking to his skin like painted streaks. He could have been an apparition—a figment of her imagination.

She didn't even get one of the fleeting, distracted smiles he threw her way sometimes. Especially after one of the nights when they'd had sleep sex.

* * *

"Sleep sex? He attacked you, you mean."

Charlie said this precisely and immediately, with her strawberry-red mouth perked inquisitively and her bright blue eyes focused sharply on Lucy. Across their shared desk, between file stacks and pots of mini-crocuses and the leaning tower of ring binders, her words spread like a coffee spill.

"No! We both did it. I mean, neither of us was more...we just...I was dreaming, and then we woke up..."

"Fucking?"

George at the window desk lifted his disheveled head and Lucy gave Charlie a kick under the table.

"Yes. If you want to call it that."

"Well, darling, it isn't crochet. So tell me. How often."

"Two, maybe three times. Is it bad, do you think? Should we see someone?"

"A doctor, you mean?" Charlie shrugged. "A counselor, maybe. I don't know. It depends."

"On what?"

She raised one very well-plucked eyebrow and bit the end of her pen with small, square white teeth. "Was it any good?"

The question was immaterial, but Lucy didn't quite know how to say so. Sex with her and John wasn't good or bad, something to award three and a half stars to—one for technique and two for effort and a half for the pillow talk afterward.

When she—well, when she and John *crocheted*—it was a communication. Not a performance. It was how they talked to each other. Or used to, before life got so tangled up and frazzled. They were trying to reach each other, his cock in her and his fingers on her and her hands in his hair—she didn't know if Charlie would understand. The sleep sex wasn't like that. It started in unconsciousness, with deep and dark and hot, meaty dreams, and she woke to find her body screwing John's, yes fucking it, like animals, silent and eyes shut, their hot mouths pressed together and the sheets pushed roughly aside.

"I don't know," Lucy said to Charlie, throwing a blue folder onto the pile where she put things she didn't know where to file. "Yes. Better than nothing, I suppose."

"Ah. Bit of a drought?"

"Not a drought. Some other kind of natural disaster. A long, complicated one with dementia and packed lunches and laundry and shouting."

"Oh, those. I think they call them life. Always done my best to avoid it."

Charlie smirked, but Lucy caught the seesaw in her voice and noticed how she put her pen down carefully beside her keyboard, her lipstick slightly smudged.

"I'm not complaining. I know I'm lucky," Lucy said.

"So lucky it makes you want to weep?"

Lucy looked up. She shrugged. "Only if I could do it somewhere soft and dark and quiet with no interruptions for around three weeks."

"You need a break," Charlie said, shaking her head.

"Yes."

As Lucy watched, a soft stripe of sunlight grew slowly stronger and crawled across the desk.

"When did we last have sex?" John had asked, about six months before when the summer was spoiling outside and they were juggling chores in the falling-apart house.

"Sex?"

"Yeah, you know. When a man and a woman like each other very much..."

"Shut up." She threw a leek at him. She was cooking lunch,

soup, because it seemed wholesome and soothing, even though nobody ate much of it and it made such a mess. Her mother was sitting next door watching a video with the kids and nobody was screaming yet. She'd almost thought she could breathe. And then he hit her with his absurd question.

"John."

"Lucy."

"It's the last thing on my mind. You know, things have been difficult."

"Since the dawn of time. And yet."

"Maybe if you didn't have to work."

"And maybe if we didn't have to feed the kids."

"Not this again."

"No. Not again. Not anymore."

He walked away, his broad shoulders a little rolled forward, his head bowed. She stood there with a knife and a celery stick in her hands and the horrible feeling that something had snapped, something irreparable.

When she first met him, she could hardly believe he'd go for her—an awkwardly tall, mousy-haired girl. She was allergic to the spotlight, and he was so at ease, so bright and strong and vivid, with that dirty-blonde hair and that dangerous smile.

Now, she wondered again why on earth he had chosen her—out of the women that seemed to flock around him, the prettier ones and the richer ones, the clever university girls and the laughing, fast-moving crowd that he hung out with.

And now, years later, she'd watched him that morning taking his tool case out of the van and shifting boxes of cables around. There was a new slackness to his cheek she hadn't noticed before. Shadows under his eyes. His aging shocked her even more than her own. For the first time, the thought hit her with a bump—even he won't live forever.

She wiped her hands and looked at the clock. Time for work.

That had been six months ago, and since then, she'd started to avoid looking at him as much as she avoided the mirror. What was the point? She focused on what had to be done.

Later in the afternoon, as the winter day leaked the last of its meager light into the kitchen, she slipped into a half-formed daydream. Stacking glasses in the dishwasher she thought of being stretched out on a beach somewhere, lying in the icing-sugar-soft sand, nothing but the sound of waves and the sun, her skin slowly turning golden.

"Mum, Nanny's outside."

"Oh?"

"She doesn't have any shoes on."

Stephen, still chewing one of the sweets that turned his mouth lurid pink and rotted his teeth, was looking over the wreckage of the kitchen table. Outside the window that framed their frozen back lawn his grandmother stood in a long, white nightgown that was bobbled under the arms and wet at the hem. The old woman's bare feet were shining with melted frost, and she was reaching to the bird table with an enraptured look on her face.

"Oh, shit," John said, barging past so fast he sent Lucy spinning. "Are you just going to stand there?" A frown was digging its way between his eyebrows and already he was outside, letting the door slam behind him. Lucy stood and gazed out at the garden.

Like watching a film. John took her mother's arm and turned her toward the front door of the granny flat. Sometimes the old woman mistook him for her long-dead husband, sometimes her own father. Now, she was taking tiny steps and frowning at her feet, as if she'd just realized that the cold was hurting. John suddenly bent and scooped her up, lifting her as if she was as light as a cat. Her hands clutched his shoulders, the blue veins and fine bones showing through paper-white skin.

"Daddy's carrying Nanny back to her house, look!" Robin pointed at the scene and knocked juice into her lap.

"Watch what you're doing, Bobbin." The child's tiny, pink face started to crumple. "Damn it. I'm sorry. It's okay. It's okay." Lucy leaned over to lift things away from the spillage, stroked her daughter's glossy hair, apologized.

John opened the back door, knocked the snow off his boots. A draft of cold air blew in with him. Once, she thought, he might have laughed, shivered, rubbed his hands. Turned it all into a silly adventure.

"Close the door, Daddy," Stephen said.

"Give me a minute," snapped John, and before she could say anything, Stephen had scrambled down from his chair and run full tilt to his room, high spots of color on his cheeks.

While the kids argued up and down the stairs and Mother went to bed early with a book—she read the same hardback poetry collection over and over—Lucy moved across the kitchen to touch her husband. She reached for his neck, and he flinched.

"It's only me," she said, pretending to tickle him.

"Not now," he said, shrugging her off. She felt a blush rise. Ridiculous. How could she blush, this man she'd lived with for a third of her life, who'd seen her give birth twice, who'd dealt with the aftermath? Besides, he had his back to her.

"Can't I touch you?" she asked.

"Seems that way." His voice was low and quiet. This was all wrong.

"John?"

He stopped brushing the dirt off his boots and let his hands rest on the edges of the sink.

"I can't do this, Lucy."

"Do what? Clean your shoes? What next—you want me to blow your nose for you?"

She was trying, but her voice was failing.

"This. Us. What we're doing. Or what we aren't."

She forced a laugh.

"Is this about the sex again?"

He looked down into the sink, at the chips and flakes of mud and grit. His jaw worked.

"It's...just for now. Things will change."

"That is true," he nodded, still looking into the sink like he was reading tea leaves. "Lucy, life goes by."

He looked up at her, then. His eyes, blue as a willow-pattern plate, flecked with gold, his long lashes. Even then, when her heart was starting to hurt quite badly, the beauty of him was stunning.

"Mummy, where are my shoes?" Robin ran into the room and slammed against her mother, hanging from her shirt.

"Not now, love," she said, pushing her daughter back toward the stairs. "Look in your room."

"Speaking of rooms."

"I'm sorry?"

"I can't sleep in there another night."

"Our bed? We don't sleep anyway, so—"

"Lucy. Please." He pressed his lips together. The room looked weird. Everything was placed wrong, like a stranger's house. The Dutch-blue walls. She struggled to focus. It hurt to stay present, but something in her was screaming, and she thought that for once, maybe she had no choice.

"I wake up sometimes and I don't know how it all happened. I'm lying there next to you and you're in that fucking dressing gown."

"In case she wakes up. Or the kids, one or the other. Christ, John, you know why."

"And I don't even recognize you." She lifted her head, startled. He was looking at her and it was actually painful, she could feel cold anger in her belly.

This wasn't John. The man who thought he could take on the world, including her mother's snobbish relations, and not only charm them but make them happy at the same time.

"I—I love you."

"You love everything day in day out without even thinking about it. It's your job."

"Are you sneering at me?"

He didn't answer. The rage rose in her like something out of control, like an animal finally driven out of its hibernating place. She heard the kids arguing next door and the front door opened and her mother's gentle, bewildered face floated in, looking at her like she'd seen a ghost she didn't quite recognize.

Lucy turned and ran. Ran to the bedroom, and threw herself in among the crumpled sheets and the clothes and the mess. The door opened and without looking to see who it was, she screamed over her shoulder.

"Get out. Leave me alone."

There was the crack of a door closing, Stephen's voice raised short and sharp. She waited for the wails, and the kids to burst in, and her mother to start saying, "Excuse me," over and over again, voice spiraling, as she did when she got distressed. They never left her alone. Never had, not for years. She buried her face in the pillow and felt her own hot breath absorbed by the feathers.

And then they did. The house that was never quiet became suddenly, weirdly so. She could hear a voice, murmuring, moving back and forth. Footsteps. Doors closing, gently. Outside the car's engine started up and she lifted her head. Where was he going? Was he taking the children? She stumbled out of bed, ran to the window, clawed back the blind. Outside it was gathering dusk, the sky stained the color of strong tea.

"John!" She practically screamed it, voice strangled.

"I'm here," he said, from behind her, and she jerked like she'd got an electric shock.

"The children—"

"Are with Sarah."

"But she never babysits at short notice."

"Now she has."

"My mother."

"With Missus Sweet, over the road."

"Is she okay? Her pills."

He shrugged. "She's as well as she can be, and she can have her pills later." He looked at her then, and the blue of his eyes was soft and warm.

"Let go."

She looked at her hands, the off-white curtains bunched in them.

"Let go." He crossed to her, but instead of bundling her into his arms and holding her, he gripped her shoulders and pulled her to the mirror. She tried to turn, but he held her fast, facing their dual reflection, shadowy and awkward.

"Look at us."

She made a face. John remained impassive, his eyes traveling slowly over her, from head to foot. This was silent torture, and immediately she started to squirm, shaking her hair over her face, reaching for the door. He gripped her wrists.

"We don't have time for this," she said, tugging away.

"I've made time. I've bought us"—he glanced at the clock— "two hours."

She heard herself bark a laugh. "If only," she said. "Trouble is we're in deficit, John, so two hours is a drop in the—"

"Enough."

His voice was low and quiet, but it fell like a curtain.

"It's enough. We need to talk, Lucy."

She looked at the drawn-out curve of his mouth and the new, faint wrinkles that beamed from the corners of his eyes like a kid's drawing of sunshine. Behind them, the day was fading. Her heart was thrumming in her chest, and she could feel the ache of tiredness in her wrists and neck.

"No." she shook her head. "No, we don't."

He frowned.

This time, when she turned, he didn't try to stop her. Keeping her eyes fixed on his, she brushed a lock of hair out of his eyes.

"Talking won't help. We don't need arguments or explanations. This, this is what we need," she said, relieved to find her voice steady. She thumbed John's lower lip. Prized his mouth open. He leaned in toward her, and although she could practically taste the kiss, she stilled him.

"Wait."

What changed, in that moment, so that a woman who couldn't even look at her own reflection stood back and started to strip herself naked? Maybe she let go, like he'd suggested. Maybe for a minute she stopped thinking long enough for the glimmer of her feelings to start to show. And there wasn't a trace of shame or worry, as she unbuttoned her blouse and skirt and dropped them on the floor. Maybe it was the turning of the year at last—by the time she'd pulled off her knickers and tramped them onto the carpet, unhooked her bra and felt the sigh of relief as her soft, naked self glowed in the half light, she didn't really care.

"Now, you," she said quietly, and reached to undo John's

shirt. He stood and let her do it. She unbuckled his belt and tugged at his trousers, smelling the good soap and body smell of his skin, feeling the heat of it as she drew close. He stepped out of his shoes, and looked for a moment like a boy who didn't know what to do next.

She loved him for that. It gave her the confidence to sink onto her knees, and hug him, pressing her face into his groin, burying her cheek in his pubic hair and brushing against his half-stiff cock. For a few minutes, they stayed like that, holding each other, his hands combing her hair and the two of them rocking slightly. She could feel his knees against her breasts and his anklebone slide between her legs.

"Feels so good," he murmured, and it did. She could have stayed there forever, exchanging warmth, reveling in the pleasure like a warm bath. Only other impulses were starting to gather, from somewhere far away. Her knees were weakening at the familiar, delightful feel of his skin on hers. And every time he rocked, his cock moved a little closer to her mouth and her clit slid against his ankle. She nuzzled into his groin. Felt the silky skin against her lips.

One of the things she loved about John was the noise he made in bed. Those low moans, the soft, emphatic swear words, were enough to make her wet without even touching him. Now, as she took the head of his cock in her mouth and sucked it hard, he whimpered as though he were almost in pain.

"Oh god, Lucy, please," he said.

She flicked her tongue back and forth over the globe of his glans, and smiled.

"I like it when you beg," she said, grabbing his hand and pulling him to the floor beside her. She needed to feel him intensely, intimately—there was a feeling like the tiniest flame between her legs and it had to be paid attention, coaxed into life.

"I want your tongue on me." She pulled his hand to the place she wanted it. "Right here. Lick me." She felt herself blush as she said it—these were not the kind of words she'd exchanged with her husband for as long as she could remember—if ever. Not sober, not out loud. But she kept going, and the nerves only seemed to make her bolder. Lit up the blood in her veins. As John knelt in front of her and slid the point of his very skilled tongue right between the lips of her pussy, she kept talking.

"Yes, yes, yes."

He worked at her, lightly and with total concentration. Every so often, he would pull back and look up at her, that strange new frown still darkening his brow. And she would grip his hair and move him back into place, to feel that sweet, sweet tongue on her again.

"Keep going, baby."

At last, he pulled back, pushing their discarded clothes aside, tossing stray pieces of Lego and odd shoes across the room, clearing a space. He shoved her knees apart, and she grabbed him by the hips. They were moving fast now, no longer tender.

"No need to rush," she said, warning him. "Two hours."

He barked a laugh. "Unlikely. I think I'd implode."

"Make it last," she said. "I want to feel every minute with you, John."

Then he stopped. She saw his eyes dull. "Why d'you say that?"

"Why do you think? I've needed this for so long. Missed it." She ran a hand down the hard, sculpted curves of his arm, over the softer skin of his belly. She knew his body so well, but it was a revelation every time she unwrapped it and saw it naked. Now, she noticed a new scratch on his side—from fixing the fence last week, and how the hairs on his chest were starting to spring up white instead of brown. The way his shoulders were starting to curve.

"You make it sound like it's the last time."

Her eyes widened. She buried her hand in the scribble of his pubic hair and held on tight.

"God, I hope not. Not yet."

His shoulders relaxed, and he shook his head. A smile broke out on his mouth and he closed his eyes, let himself lean into her hand.

"Lucy. I never know what's going on in your head."

"That makes two of us," she said, working her hand lower, reaching for his erection. It had faded a little, but she felt him leap under her touch. "Most of the time I'm just getting through the days."

"I thought you'd…"

"What?"

He sighed. "Stopped. Wanting me."

"Are you mad?" she fastened on his cock tighter than she'd meant to, saw him jolt a bit.

"Sorry."

"It's okay. No, don't stop. Please. And no, I'm not mad, just tired and sleep deprived and confused, and it may be the same thing." His voice was starting to break as she worked his cock nearer to her, pulling him in to her body and spreading her legs wide.

"Imagine waking up with you," she said, whispering into his ear, now, as he positioned himself and held her hips, pressed the head of his cock against her slit. She groaned at the resistance, and her breath caught in her throat when he drove into her, sliding fast as he met the wetness inside her. "Every day. That's what I thought."

"Huh? When?"

She looked at him, held his chin in her hands and met his gaze. His eyelids were half closing as he slid his cock in and out of her, his mouth open and his breath coming fast.

"When I first started seeing you," she said, struggling to keep talking, refusing to drop eye contact. "I felt like I was dreaming."

"God, Lucy, I've wanted you."

"Shhh. Listen."

She tensed her legs, caught his hips and stopped him from moving. He tried to thrust, but she held him fast and they laughed.

"I thought we didn't need to talk?" He leaned in to nip at her throat with his teeth.

"I'm not talking. I'm trying to work something out. This is important, babe."

"Okay." He nodded, relaxed. Held himself steady for a minute. "I'm listening."

"Everything was so good it seemed like something out of a dream, a book. And I would imagine how it would be to live with you, you know, be close all the time."

"Cause I was never allowed to stay over." He sank into her, a smile curled in the corner of his mouth. She relaxed her legs and drew him in, pressed the small of his back.

"Close?" he asked.

"Mm-hm. But I thought—how will it be when we're really living, once we're married, parents, in a house, once we're... grown-up."

"Oh, god—I'm listening, I'm listening," he said, moving his hips so slowly and deep that it felt like her lower half was dissolving with intense pleasure. "But I can't help fucking you, okay?"

"Yes. Don't stop."

For a minute they were silent, reveling in each other's bodies, how they fitted together so well, how good it felt to be so close again. Outside the day had sunk into darkness, and Lucy thought how clean and black and absolute it was—how certain. She lay on the floor with her husband and thought of the things she knew for certain. Who she loved. What her body needed. That things would change, whatever happened, the days would pass—shorter or longer.

John shifted, and held her in place, and she could tell from the catch in his breath that he was close to coming.

"And now we're there, grown-up, and I feel like I'm half-asleep. I went from dreaming to half-asleep."

"And now?" John moaned. He held her by the hips and thrust deep.

"Now, I want to wake up with you," she said, slipping her hand between them, feeling the quickening and the bloom of the orgasm. "I want to be here."

"Here?"

"Yes. Now. Now. I want to be with you, and know it, and live wide awake. Right here. Every moment. Good and bad."

He nodded his head and looked at her straight on, his blue and white eyes as bright as a sudden summer's day in midwinter. His body drove into hers and locked there. She smiled. He said, "Okay."

And they came.

A COMPETITIVE MARRIAGE

Victoria Blisse

I looked out of the window on a gray Mancunian winter's evening. It was pitch black and the pools of egg yolk–yellow streetlights showed it was still raining, the ripples impacting the puddles left from days of the same kind of weather.

"I'm not going out there tonight," I said, shaking my head. "No way, it's too cold and wet and miserable."

"All right, love," was my husband's chirpy reply. He was on his laptop, deeply involved in tending to imaginary vegetation or flinging some poor animated animal to its doom.

"I hate to miss my exercise, though. The wedding is only a few months away."

"Do something on the Wii, then. Exercise indoors."

"Oh, now that's a good plan."

I'd been walking every day since my sister announced she was getting married and wanted me, her older sister, to be a bridesmaid. It had sent me into a spiral of panic, worried I would look more like the wedding cake than the cake itself, or I'd be the size of the other two bridesmaids put together.

So I decided to lose some weight by walking every day and attempting to eat right. The walking was pleasant when I started in the early autumn sun, the crunching of crisp leaves and the scent of bonfires and nature on the air. By the time Christmas arrived it was less pleasant, though I did enjoy walking in the cool crisp snow, the only sound the crunch of my boots, the world a soft blanket of white around me.

I was ready for winter to be over, though. We were securely into the new year but not quite deep enough to be seeing signs of spring, and the incessant rain got me down. I'd come back in from my walks cold, wet and grumpy. I couldn't face it again.

The Wii had been a Christmas present for the lads, Jake and Charlie, who had played nicely with it so far. They'd have a remote each and sometimes they'd play racing games and other times they'd be up and bopping to music. I'd watched them several times but never felt the urge to join in. The little men were in bed and sound asleep, both ready for another busy day at infant school the next morning, so it was all mine.

The first challenge was switching the damn thing on.

"It's the long, thin button on the front." My husband's calm and slightly amused voice carried from behind his laptop.

"Thank you dear, I've got it." I smiled triumphantly. Nothing happened on the TV screen even though the little light on the game box thing turned green.

"Hang on, I need to change the TV channel."

Again, Ian came to my rescue. He did it a lot; we'd been married for ten years and he'd always been my geek in holographic armor. We met in a music store. He was playing on one of those daft games; I was looking for the latest Take That album and not looking where I was going. I backed into him, he yelled at me for getting him killed and from there love blossomed.

"Urgh, Ian, I don't know what I'm doing here," I finally admitted. "Can you help me?"

He sighed a little impatiently, still engrossed in his computer screen.

"Please?" I added, with a cute pout and one of those looks, the ones I'd always used to get my way.

"Oh, go on then," he sighed. "What do you want to play?"

"That dancey one the boys bop about to."

"Well, you grab it off the side. I'll just finish up in my game."

I looked through the plastic packs until I found one that had the word *dance* on it.

"Got it," I crowed, "What now?"

Ian put down his laptop and shook his head.

"You're going to have to join us in the computer age sooner or later, dear," he chuckled and took the game out of my hand.

"Well, I can Google, what else do I need?" I was very good at Googling in fact. I'd got many bargains online, cheap shoes and bags for me and the weird geekery stuff all my boys, including my husband, liked to receive for birthdays and Christmas and such. "I've got you for all the other stuff."

Ian laughed and bent to put the game in the machine. He also picked the remotes up from their position beside the box and passed one to me.

"Slip it around your right wrist and tighten the strap," he said, "then I'll get you started."

"Don't you want to play?" It had just hit me how daft I'd look prancing around the living room. I didn't want Ian behind me, giggling or even worse recording me on his phone to send into *You've Been Framed*.

"I've got to get my cabbages—"

"Fuck your bloody pretend brassicas, mate. Come on, play with me. Please?"

My darling husband's face was set in its determined line. The one he used for denying the boys one more game of Mario before bed. "I don't want to, Manda. I've never played that game, I'm no good at dancing."

"Aw, come on. I'm crap at dancing too. I tell you what, we'll make it a competition."

I saw a light come on in his eyes. Ian was very competitive. I've got him to do so many things by turning them into a contest. Cleaning, shopping, visiting my relatives. It was amazing what I could turn into a game if I had to.

"Go on then, what kind of contest?"

"Well, a wager," I replied, "best of—I dunno—three games wins."

"Wins what?" He added.

Often the bribery would involve the removal of a chore from his list or a promise to make his favorite dessert that night. This time, I decided on something a little more fun.

"An orgasm."

"Oh," he said, brightening up, "sounds good."

"Yeah, winner receives one full orgasm from the other competitor with no need to return the favor, redeemable at any time up to six months, no purchase necessary."

Ian chortled. It's a great sound that gets me in the pit of my stomach still, and I must have heard it a million times over the years. My man is sexy, though. I can't help myself.

"Okay, Mandy, you're on."

It really was a win-win situation. I would love to be showered with all his sexual prowess, but I would be equally happy to suck his cock until he came. I'm rather easy like that. Ian makes me that way; he's hot. I want to touch him all the time;

our friends are always complaining about our inappropriate touching in public. I couldn't help it though. I wanted to wind my fingers through his or pinch his cute little bubble butt or run my fingers down his hard chest. I enjoyed reaching up to nuzzle his neck or his lips or cheek. I enjoyed being pulled into his body, snuggled beside my man.

"Okay." Ian's voice woke me from my daydream. "Do you know what you're doing?"

"Not a clue," I answered.

"Just hold your remote like this." He held it in his hand like a relay racer holds the baton. "And move about. You don't have to press any buttons."

"I can do that." I nodded and gripped my plastic stick accordingly.

"Right, I've set it to randomly pick songs for us so there'll be no fighting."

"Okay, boss." I winked cheekily, and he reached out his left hand to slap at my bottom.

"Less of that, you," he growled. He did it on purpose; he knew that tone of voice made me wet.

"Sorry, sir," I responded, and pressed a kiss to his cheek.

"No distracting me, you little minx. Now, are you ready?"

"Yes—I mean no. Not yet. Hang on."

I took off the zipped-up jogging top I'd put on to go outside in. Beneath it was a light, white T-shirt.

"I'll still be too hot," I said. "I was dressed for the outdoors."

I slipped off my T-shirt and stood proudly in my plain white sports bra. I'd not reveal so much flesh to anyone else ever, but I knew Ian would appreciate it.

"Two can play this game," he said and set to pulling down his jeans. If he was going to bring out the arse, so was I. I kicked off my trainers and my thick cotton trousers followed. I was clad in just my underwear, all my curves revealed. I looked over to Ian. He was stripped down to his boxer-briefs, the ones with a picture of Animal from the Muppets on them that I'd bought him for Christmas. I loved to indulge his playful side.

"Right, now are you ready?" he asked, leisurely running his gaze up and down my body.

"Yep, I'm ready. Bring it on." I parted my legs and bounced up and down on the balls of my feet in what I hoped was a stance similar to that engaged in by the All Blacks rugby team. It didn't seem to intimidate Ian though. He just cocked his head to look at my arse.

Just then the music sprang into life, and I had to concentrate on the telly. Did I mention I am just a little bit clumsy? Well I am, and I'm not so very coordinated at all. Ian effortlessly moved in time with the beat while I was still working out which foot to put forward first. Partway through the second chorus I went right when I should have gone left and bumped my hip into his.

"Cheat," he exclaimed.

"Sorry," I yelled, "I didn't mean to."

I didn't have time in the first song to appreciate the wonder of my man moving with such fluidity and rhythm clad in the bare minimum of clothing. As he bounded up and down when the screen announced the winner of the first round, I let myself indulge in a little ogling. His hard thighs, his lithe chest, even the cute little pouch of his stomach that showed how much he loved my cooking. I loved every inch of him but especially those inches hidden from my sight.

"Ready for round two, loser?" he taunted.

"Pride comes before a fall, mate, so watch it." I bent myself, ready for the next challenge, and as I focused on the screen before me I felt the impact of my husband's hand on my arse, making me totter forward.

"Bastard," I yelled, as the song burst onto the screen and I struggled to keep up.

He just smirked. The sting of my buttock distracted me at first. I wanted to just turn the game off in a huff and make him spank me for being a bad girl. I nearly did it too, but then I noticed something. I knew the song and the dance moves to it. I cackled gleefully and set myself back in time to my disco days and love of the Spice Girls. Soon I was lighting up perfects on every move. Ian was not impressed.

"Always knew my extensive knowledge of disco dance moves would prove an advantage in life." It was my turn to smirk as I was pronounced winner.

"A fluke," he said. "You're still going down, missus."

"Oh no, darling, you are." I ran my fingers down my body and hooked my thumb into my cotton knickers and pulled the elastic down, just enough to show a flash of public hair. Ian was engrossed and missed the action on the telly. I snapped the knickers back and started to move along with the character on the screen.

Ian cursed and joined in a moment later than me. I concentrated on following the action and realized that maybe I was as competitive as my husband. I pushed myself to my limit, but still I was not coordinated enough to actually successfully complete each movement. Ian's score soared past mine so I decided desperate times called for desperate measures.

"Ian," I cried. He looked toward me and I lifted up my bra, freeing my boobs. He stumbled, his jaw dropped and I just wiggled my right hand with the remote in it in hope that by sheer coincidence I might gain a few more points.

He cursed and looked away from me to check the scores.

I held my breath as the song finished and the little game imps or whatever it was calculated the final score, and then groaned loudly when it was revealed.

"Yes!" Ian punched the air then wiggled his butt. "I won!"

I growled and crossed my hands across my chest.

"Oh, no, don't hide 'em baby. I'm taking my prize now. Get here."

I dropped my arms to the side of my body and he pulled me tightly to him. He ravaged my lips with his, plundering my mouth and squeezing my breasts against his chest. I'm not a sore loser, and how could this be a bad thing anyway? I prayed the boys would sleep soundly, listening carefully for the creak of the stairs that could give away them making their way to us.

Ian was lost in the moment so it was good that I was paying attention. He pushed down on my hips to indicate I should kneel. My pussy clenched and I gratefully sank to my knees. We're somewhat equal in day-to-day matters, maybe even I'm slightly more dominant, but when it came to sex Ian was definitely the guy on top, even when I was riding him. He liked to be in control; I liked to let him take over although sometimes I'd protest, just to make him growl and narrow his eyes. I liked to be his naughty girl.

But a bet was a bet, and I owed him one orgasm. When I settled on my knees in our thankfully thick-pile carpet I hooked my fingers into his pants and pulled them down to skim his knees. He was hard and straining. I loved his darkened rod, the bulbous top, the long straight lines leading down to his tight, crinkled balls. I shuffled forward a touch, rested my hands on his thighs and pressed my lips to the very tip of his cock.

I looked up into his intense stare. He wrapped his hand in my ponytail, ready to push me if he needed to, but it was just a show of his dominance; I didn't need any further encouragement. I slipped my lips around him and followed gravity. I took in just his head at first, swirled my tongue around its soft, rounded shape, tickling at that spot where it met the shaft, eliciting a growl from him. He tightened his fingers in my hair as I lifted up and sank down again. I took a little more of his stiffened flesh into my mouth and bobbed up and down a few times consecutively, enjoying the light friction of my lips against his dick.

I sucked with great verve and passion and while I did, slipped my right hand from his thigh to the juncture of mine. Sometimes he'd be cruel and tell me I couldn't masturbate while I pleased him, but still I had to try. The ache in my clit couldn't be ignored.

I looked up when I ran my fingers inside my knickers and saw how involved in my blow job Ian was. His head was stretched back, his eyes closed, his jaw clenched tight. I couldn't count how many times I'd sucked him in the fifteen years we'd been together, but it still got to him, still aroused him to such a level that he had to fight not to come too soon. It thrilled me. When I rubbed at my wetted nether lips, they split eagerly around my finger. I found my clit and the rhythm to stroke it that pleased me most. I nodded my head in time, and Ian moaned loudly.

I knew he was going to come; I felt the throb of his erection, the taste of his salty secretion and the tension in his leg muscles as he braced himself for that release. I rubbed my tongue down the underside of his shaft as I bobbed, and labored to keep the pace steady, eager to please him and to feel his warm come fill my mouth.

"Fuck, Mand, gonna come." He tightened his fist in my hair and I kept my lips around him. I wanted to taste him this time even though, ever the gentleman, he'd warned me in case I wanted it elsewhere. He grunted and stilled, and his come squirted into my mouth, coated it and sat heavily on my tongue.

I lapped and sucked and relished it. He tasted musky, a hint of earthy mushroom tinged with the sweetness of apple.

He stroked my hair, and I stroked my sticky clit. I let my mouth hang loosely around him, tasting him, feeling him soften in my mouth. I was close to coming; as my thighs tightened I prayed they wouldn't cramp up as my orgasm blossomed.

"Come for me," he whispered. I knew he was watching me, knew he'd read the signs, knew he wanted me to feel pleasure too. I came, my body wracked with electrical spasms turned up so high the voltage went from pain to pleasure while my mind was wrapped up in the comfort and ecstasy of his love.

It was the next day when I found out Ian hadn't been quite truthful with me. When I told the boys I'd played their dance game with Daddy the night before, they both told me how good at it he was, how they often played it together when they got in from school on those nights I was on the late shift at work.

Maybe Ian had been right; maybe it was time for me to enter the computer age and beat him at his own game. Yeah, maybe I was just a little competitive too.

PROFESSIONAL, KNOWLEDGEABLE AND VERY THOROUGH

Annabeth Leong

"Tamara, can you come out to the front?"

Tamara Owens sighed and worked her head a little closer to the engine she was currently examining. "It's the '97 Civic, right? I knew that guy would be upset."

Her service consultant's heels clicked against the garage's concrete floor. Pacing. Never a good sign. "I think you should come out here. He keeps insisting he just had the timing belt serviced six months ago, and he doesn't trust anything I say."

She couldn't avoid this. Tamara emerged from the engine reluctantly, wiping grease from her fingers with a soiled rag. "Hell, Lucy, you could practically fix the damn thing yourself if you didn't have better things to do. What am I going to tell him that you can't?" Tamara hated talking to customers, who tended to question her and ask for the boss (sometimes even refusing to believe that she was the boss). She trained her service consultants exhaustively in customer service, parts and mechanics to avoid exactly this situation.

Lucy shrugged helplessly, her blonde ringlets bobbing around her ears. "Would you please just come?"

Tamara resisted the urge to growl and throw a tool to the ground. Childish behavior like that wasn't exactly uncommon in the business—separate people worked the front desk for a very good reason—but as with all things, Tamara felt she had to hold herself to a higher standard in order to maintain respect. Not for the first time, she considered hiring a man to wear overalls and talk to customers for her. "I'll be there in a second," she said. Casting a longing glance over her shoulder, where the engine gleamed dully with its straightforward problems, Tamara headed to the sink to clean up and collect herself.

The sight of the tall, sharply dressed man waiting beside the counter did nothing to improve Tamara's mood. Everything about him spoke of precision, from his tailored suit to his obviously gym-perfected musculature to his smooth shave and gleamingly polished shoes. He was way too handsome, way too expensive and Tamara could just tell how miserable he was about to make her.

Most of the time she could accept being halfway presentable, along with all her other halfways—halfway strong, halfway slim, halfway respected, halfway making a living with her business, halfway between her white Mississippi mother and black Massachusetts father. A man like this, who seemed to know exactly who to be and where to stand, made Tamara feel she had gotten halfway to nowhere.

She cleared her throat and summoned her most professional voice. "Sir? My service consultant tells me you asked to speak to the mechanic who'd be working on the car." Tamara braced for condescension—maybe he'd ask to speak to the actual mechanic, or request a different mechanic take over the job. Instead, he surprised her.

He shook her hand with a firm grip—his palm was softer than hers—and introduced himself. "Randal Dean. Look, I'm sorry to make you leave your work. I just don't understand this thing about the timing belt. I had service done on that six months ago, and now you guys are telling me I need to do it again. Did my other mechanic screw me over? Are you guys looking to take advantage of a guy who doesn't know a timing belt from a...um...from a steering wheel? What's going on here?"

Tamara blinked. His sheepish smile revealed gorgeous dimples in his cheeks that gave boyish appeal to what might otherwise have been a clipped, businesslike tone. A very slight accent tipped her off to his Chinese heritage, making her reinterpret her initial read of his light-skinned features. He met her eyes directly, with respect, neither slipping in incredulous glances at her tool belt nor straying down to her breasts to check her out. For once, a little part of her wished he would show some awareness of her curves. She certainly noticed his refined good looks and the masculine perfection of his body's lines.

Pushing down her unexpected arousal, Tamara attempted to focus on the problem at hand. "Lucy should have explained the situation to you. You've got oil leaking from your cam seals. If that gets onto your timing belt, it doesn't matter if it's new. The fluid could degrade the belt—either by eating it, or just by saturating it and causing it to slip." She stopped talking when Randal shook his head vigorously.

"I need you to slow way, way down," he said. "Explain it to me like I'm a three-year-old. Tell me why I need to pay hundreds of dollars for timing belt service twice in a very short time." He paused and raked a hand through his hair, flashing a grin. "It wouldn't hurt if you could also explain what the hell a timing belt is."

Tamara took a deep breath and tried again. "A timing belt

helps coordinate your crank and cam shafts," she began.

"You lost me already."

Now Tamara could understand Lucy's problem. Randal Dean might not be the kind of sexist jerk she'd been expecting, but he was a piece of work in his own right. "With all due respect, Randal, it took me a long time to learn how a car works. I want to answer your questions and make sure you feel comfortable about how you're spending your money with us, but at a certain point, you do have to trust my professional opinion. I've got a lot of other cars to fix. I can't give you a long lesson right now." She sighed, summoning a phrase from the customer service training she'd attended herself. "What can I do to help resolve this issue?"

"Can I come back later?" he asked, and something about his tone heated Tamara's cheeks. "When you're less busy and you can spend a little time?"

She bit the inside of her cheek. Her day was booked solid, and this wouldn't be quick. To accommodate his request, she'd definitely have to stay late. Still, something inside her hesitated to tell him no.

"Five o'clock," she said. "Lucy will be closing up. The car will be ready by then, and I'll walk you through everything I did, show you the parts I replaced, the works. We can just hang out in the garage until you're satisfied." She stumbled over the last word of her sentence. It conjured an image of a different sort of satisfaction, sweaty and messy and delicious. Tamara envisioned straddling Randal and running a grease-stained finger across his smooth, high cheekbone, leaving a smear behind. She wondered what it would be like to get him dirty. Coughing a little, Tamara tried to clear the fantasy from her mind.

A faint smile spreading across his face suggested his mind had traveled to a similar place. He remained professional, however, promising to be prompt and pay for the demand on her time.

She watched Lucy lead Randal to her car, preparing to drop him off wherever he needed to be between now and five. Tamara's sense of foreboding hadn't diminished in the slightest—it had only changed. That man was still much too handsome, much too expensive and much too tempting.

Randal returned at precisely five o'clock. Tamara told Lucy to send him back to the garage, and to stick around for at least another hour in case he turned out to be a creep.

He greeted Tamara with a businesslike handshake, though she thought his palm might have lingered in hers a beat longer than necessary. For the next hour, she described a timing belt's function at length, detailing how its failure could cause valves and pistons inside the engine to interfere with each other to disastrous effect. She explained that even a new timing belt could be destroyed by an oil leak. Then she showed him the dried cam seals she'd removed from his car's engine.

To be honest, the worn rubber rings she'd discovered had shocked her. She held them up for his inspection. "See how cracked, brittle and hard those things are?" Tamara asked. "Whoever replaced your timing belt should really have noticed that. It takes a lot of labor for me to get down to that part of the engine, and those parts don't cost that much. If you're already in there and you see these things look old, you might as well replace them to be safe." She tossed him a new cam seal. "See the difference? How it springs back when you pinch it? Feel it."

She picked one up herself and squeezed to demonstrate.

"It is hard," he said, imitating her movements. Her gaze snapped to him, ready to call him out for innuendo, but he met her challenging gaze with apparent innocence. He smelled great, too—his clean, spiced apple scent stood out brightly against the greasy engine smells all around them. Even without intentional provocation from Randal, Tamara's nipples stood at attention. Again, she imagined what it would be like to touch him. Would his black eyes widen with surprise when she pressed her lips to his? Would he use those muscles to grab her ass with ferocious intensity?

She rushed to cover her reaction to him. "I didn't actually replace the timing belt because the oil hadn't gotten to it yet. If you compare your bill to your estimate, you'll see we removed that charge."

As if on cue, Lucy poked her head in to check on them. Tamara smiled, glad to be free of Randal before she had to think any more about her heart's unbidden pounding. While Lucy took care of his bill, she could close up his engine and concentrate on getting him out of her life. The last thing she needed was to embarrass herself with a client.

She'd almost caught her breath when his approaching footsteps quickened it again. "Mind if I use your sink?" he asked. "I picked up some grease from that seal you showed me."

Tamara agreed, then realized she'd have to lead him to the back corner of the garage. She'd started a reorganization project there that had left the area littered with car parts and tools. The cramped space forced her to stand much closer to him than she otherwise would have. "I'm not sure how much good that will do you," she muttered, indicating the gray sliver of soap resting on the lip of the sink.

"You must have guys hitting on you all the time," Randal said suddenly as he rubbed his hands together under the fitful stream of water from the metal faucet.

Tamara blinked at the non sequitur. "What makes you think so?"

"Your confidence," Randal said. "Your skill. It's hot as hell.

And a lot of men get turned on when a woman can do a job they think of as a man's." He cleared his throat and dried his hands on the rag she kept beside the sink. "Combined with your looks, it's deadly. People must bother you pretty often." He glanced at her, desire clear in his eyes for the first time. Her body responded with a wet ache, right in her center. Tamara caught herself wondering why she didn't take him. What harm could it do to get laid?

A smile played over Tamara's lips. For once, she felt more amused than bitter. "Usually, they bother me by acting like I don't even know how to drive a car, much less repair one. I don't really have a lot of problems with being asked on dates."

Randal curled his lip, just slightly. "Stupid men."

She smirked. "Is this an elaborate way of asking me out?"

He hesitated for so long that she wondered if he would take the opportunity she'd given him. "I really shouldn't. I don't want to—"

"Bother me," Tamara finished for him.

He shrugged and spread his hands, and she saw he'd stained them again on the rag he'd used to wipe them. Tamara didn't want to resist anymore. She touched the oil streak that crossed his palm. "Are you sure you know what you're getting into? This is a pretty dirty place." To emphasize her point, she did what she'd fantasized about only hours before, tracing his cheekbone with one greasy finger. A sense of primal victory filled her chest when she stepped back and stared at the mark she'd made on his perfect, chiseled face.

For a second, Randal didn't react and Tamara worried she'd miscalculated. Then he reached for her, crushing her body to his with exactly the strength she'd hoped to feel.

"What about your suit?"

"I'll owe the dry cleaner a lot of money. It will be worth it."

He bent to kiss her, but Tamara stopped him before he could reach her lips. She felt greedy, and wanted to take him her way. "Hold on," she said. "Since you don't mind ruining your suit… stay right there."

Tamara ran to retrieve the unused timing belt from the kit she'd opened for his car. She returned and showed him the rubber belt, ridged on one side with a corrugated pattern. "As I was trying to explain," she said, "this thing synchronizes the engine valves to make sure they run smoothly."

She approached Randal and wound the belt around his hips, using it to tug him toward her. Grinning, he let her pull his body tightly against hers. His erection rubbed plainly against her pelvis. He reached between them to undo Tamara's work shirt, while she continued her feigned lecture. "We wouldn't want to disturb the rhythm between us, so it's very important to make sure this belt is tight and properly installed."

She did let Randal kiss her the next time he tried. He tasted clean and crisp and male. Tamara moaned when he pressed his tongue between her lips, then lifted her chest to grant him access.

Randal pushed up her sports bra and cupped her breasts. Despite his claims about the supposed sexiness of her job, Tamara so often felt her femininity wound up hidden or overlooked. Not so when Randal touched her. The gentle brush of his fingertips against her nipples made her feel curvy and desirable.

For the next little while, she forgot her game and gave herself over to his kisses, her grip on the timing belt loosening. Randal kissed his way down her neck and shoulder, sweeping aside the coiled hair she let run wild to reach bare skin. He dropped to his knees on the dirty concrete floor, apparently unconcerned about his suit, and kissed her stomach while undoing the fly of her worn jeans.

She shivered when he pulled her jeans down past her hips, baring her panties. She could barely remember the last time she'd had her pussy licked, and now Randal's breath heated her through her underwear.

He pressed another kiss to her clit through cotton she'd already soaked with her arousal. Then he pulled back with a slight frown.

"What's the matter?"

Mischief danced in Randal's eyes. "Well, I think you warned me that fluid could degrade the belt. I'm no expert, but I think I found a leak." His finger toyed with the elastic edges of her panties.

Tamara relaxed and grinned. She bit her lip to keep from laughing. "I don't think that part can be replaced. You'll have to plug it and see if that helps."

Randal wasted no time slipping off her underwear and sliding a finger into her wet pussy. Tamara's cunt gripped at him, pleased but unsatisfied. "That leak is bigger than that," she told him.

He took the hint and filled her with two fingers, then three. Tamara groaned and rocked against his hand. It felt good to be touched, to feel the light kisses he feathered over her inner thighs, but she wanted more. Then she remembered the timing belt still in her hand and wound it gently around the back of his head.

"We should see if these parts have been adjusted to work together correctly," she said, using the belt to guide his mouth back to her clit. Randal chuckled, but obliged, giving her a long, slow upward stroke with the flat of his tongue.

"That is perfect," Tamara moaned. "We just need to run the test long enough to…" She trailed off, unable to keep up the metaphor while he licked her and fucked her with his fingers. Her hands fisted around the rubber belt. Her oncoming orgasm made it hard for her to keep her feet.

Randal nipped her clit gently and electricity shot through Tamara's body, destroying her dexterity entirely. Her cunt pulsed. She'd never come standing up before, but she did now, so disoriented by the waves of pleasure coursing through her that she barely knew which way was up. Shaking with orgasm, she released the timing belt, not wanting to hurt him if she stumbled.

Randal caught her around the middle and held her, still stroking her. "I should have been paying more attention," he murmured against her stomach. "You did warn me that if the belt got too saturated, it could slip."

"Mmm," Tamara responded, foggy with pleasure. She was far from finished with him, though. "It's still leaking," she told him, gesturing toward her pussy.

"You're the professional," Randal said, "but I do have a special tool I could try. I don't think my fingers were big enough."

Tamara could not help giggling at the silliness of their game. "Yes, you'd better try your 'special tool.'"

Randal removed his suit jacket and spread it on the floor. Even woozy with orgasm, she reached out to stop him. "You don't have to—"

"Nonsense." He guided her onto it, then took off his shirt and folded it into a pillow for her. Tamara gazed up at him, not sure if she was more impressed by his romantic gesture or by the definition of his abs. He smiled down at her. "Now," Randal said, "I do that frantic search for the condom guys keep in their wallets just in case."

Tamara grinned. "Or we can grab my pants and check the one in my wallet. If it's not expired, that is."

Randal returned her smile and tossed her the pants. "Glad it's not just me."

Tamara produced the condom while Randal stripped to bare skin. She buried her nose against his cock, breathing in his sharp male musk, then rolled the condom over his erection. She thought of a few more funny comments about leaks and oil, but right then she wanted him too much to bother with that anymore. She lay back, spread her legs and invited him in.

Randal rested his palms on either side of Tamara's head and slid his cock into her. She rolled her hips up to welcome it, and soon discovered their timing was perfect. He advanced when she needed him deeper, then withdrew and rocked just within her entrance right at the moment she wanted to feel him there instead.

Tamara leaned up to kiss him, gripping his ass tightly and pulling him into her. She couldn't believe how smoothly he moved within her, or how perfectly he fit. Her second orgasm came to her easily, pleasure gliding through her from head to foot as she buried her face in the side of Randal's neck.

His orgasm followed a moment later. Not the noisy type, he placed his mouth against Tamara's ear to let her hear the tiny hitch his throat gave when he came. He eased his weight onto her. "You are the best mechanic," Randal whispered. "Patient, professional, knowledgeable...and very thorough."

She held him against her for a moment, savoring the experience and wondering what she ought to do next. Then she released him so he could take care of the condom. She watched his back as he walked toward the sink. Tamara decided that when he returned, she could ask him to dinner.

"Hey," Randal said lightly as he turned on the water. "You never showed me the valve cover gasket. Did that turn out to be in good shape after all?"

"It certainly wasn't dried out like the cam seals," Tamara answered, then trailed off, lifting herself onto one elbow. The facility with which he'd referred to cars as they made love took on a different cast in her mind. "Most people who can't tell a timing belt from a steering wheel wouldn't know a valve cover gasket if it put a gun to their heads." Adrenaline poured through her body, erasing the relaxation her orgasms had brought. "Who are you?"

The easy smile he'd been wearing fell off his face. He turned toward her and held up his hands. Now, his gym-sculpted body seemed to mock her.

Tamara pressed her attack. "Are you checking out the competition or something?"

"This isn't what you think," Randal said.

"I just had sex with a man who's in my place of business under false pretenses," Tamara shot back. "I'm pretty sure it's what I think." She felt too naked, too vulnerable and too embarrassed. She gathered her clothes as quickly as she could.

"Look, I'm a reporter. I'm checking out how different shops treat their customers."

She sent him a glare cold enough to freeze water. "Do I get special mention for fucking a customer?"

"Look, I know it wasn't the best thing for me to do. I tried to tell you, but... In the end, I just didn't want to stop what was happening between us. I'm sorry."

Tamara stared at him. Her body still ached with the pleasure he'd given her. She still wanted him, and she did remember the moment he'd hesitated. Tamara very nearly stretched out her arms to him, but the humiliation of being deceived burned too strongly in the back of her throat.

She turned her back on him. "You can call me later if you want, once I've had a chance to think about this. Right now, please get out."

* * *

"Can you believe he was an undercover reporter?" Lucy almost squealed the question, clearly thrilled by the glamour of the word "undercover." "'Top marks go to T.O.'s Auto Service Plus in Providence, R.I., the only shop we tried that caught every problem our test vehicle had, fixed them all and didn't charge a penny's worth of unfair parts or labor,'" she read aloud from the magazine open in her hands. She followed Tamara into the garage, ignoring her boss's every effort to retreat. "'Staff was patient, professional, knowledgeable and very thorough,'" Lucy continued.

Embarrassment flooded Tamara at the familiar phrasing. Her hands worked at her sides. Engines made so much more sense than people. "You should really keep an eye on the floor if you're going to be in here, Lucy," she said. "Especially in those heels. Why don't you put that magazine away?"

Lucy surprised her by dropping it and placing one fist on each hip instead. "What's the matter with you, Tamara? That is the best write-up we could possibly have hoped for, and in a national magazine! You'd think you would be happy! I'll even forgive Randal Dean for being such a pain in the ass while he was here."

Tamara swallowed. Lucy was right—she had no reason to be anything but delighted with the profile. She'd earned every nice thing Randal had written about her shop by being good at her job. He hadn't slipped in any patronizing words about her gender—this was definitely the first write-up she'd gotten that didn't include a line about how surprising it was that Tamara could be a competent mechanic and decently pretty woman at the very same time. As far as what had happened between them, she was the one who had sent him away. She was disappointed he hadn't called, but he didn't owe her anything.

Unfortunately, knowing that hadn't helped her get over her evening with Randal. "I just feel like he took us for a bit of a ride," she admitted to Lucy, ducking her head at her inadvertent car imagery and the memories it summoned.

"He paid us, and he gave us great press," Lucy returned brightly. "I don't know what else you want from him!" She turned on her heel and returned to the front office, leaving Tamara to stare after her. She knew exactly what else she wanted from Randal Dean, but she also knew she had no chance of getting it.

"Tamara, can you come out to the front?"

Tamara took a deep breath and emerged reluctantly from the engine she'd been working on. "Seriously, Lucy, you are probably better prepared for talking to customers than I am."

Lucy seemed exceedingly nervous this time, her fingers lacing together and unlacing in front of her body in rapid succession. "Would you please just come?"

Tamara wiped grease from her fingers, wincing a little at the way that always reminded her of Randal now. "I'll be there in a second." She cast a longing glance over her shoulder at the parts laid in a neat array on a cloth beside the car, then followed her service consultant to the front.

"I need timing belt service," a familiar voice said. "Something is leaking or something is broken—I'm not sure what it is, but I have to make it right before I suffer catastrophic engine failure."

Tamara stared. Randal stood in her front room, as sharply dressed as he'd been before, with a dozen roses in his hands. She struggled to find her voice. "Didn't you just have that service recently?"

"I should have asked my mechanic to look at the valve cover

gasket, too. My fault, really. How can she work when she doesn't know the car's whole situation? I'm hoping that sort of problem won't happen anymore once I get a permanent arrangement set up with her."

Tamara recognized his apology, and his invitation. She stepped forward and took the roses, their hands brushing together as she did. As before, he made her feel beautiful despite—or perhaps because of—all her grease and dirt.

"Can I talk to you outside?" Randal murmured when she came close.

Tamara smiled. She went behind the counter and palmed the keys to the souped-up Civic she drove herself. They would talk, certainly, and sort out anything they needed to. First, she meant to take him for a nice long ride.

RULES

Emerald

"What are you doing?"

Joyce looked up to see Pete in the doorway. "Just going through some pictures," she said, looking back down at the disorganized box in front of her. "Many of which I had forgotten I had."

Her husband moved to stand behind where she sat cross-legged on the basement floor. He squinted at the photo in her hand.

"What's that?"

Joyce laughed. "It's when I dyed my hair purple." She held it up for his better viewing.

"You dyed your hair purple?" Pete took the picture from her.

"Yeah. When I was eighteen. I told you that. Didn't I? My parents had a fit."

Pete shook his head, his eyes on the photo.

Strictly forbidden to by her parents, she recalled clearly how she'd grinned the whole time she'd sat in the salon swivel chair the day she turned eighteen, the stylist casually stripping even her light-blonde hair of its natural color—along with its natural health—to create the foundation for the vibrant hue. The picture had been taken there, right after the hairdresser had finished, by her best friend Chloe. Joyce was smiling into the camera, her shoulder-length hair a shining curtain of violet.

"Hot," Pete said now, handing the picture back to her.

Joyce laughed again. "Really?"

"Yeah." Pete smiled at her. "I like that hair-dyed-funky-color kind of look. I've always had a bit of a thing for the rebel school-girl goth character." He winked.

"You have?" This was news to her.

He shrugged. "Yeah. Nothing big—just catches my interest a bit. Plus," he paused, studying the picture over her shoulder again.

"What?"

He shrugged. "Just the attitude. It just looks like dying your hair represented something for you. I like that."

Joyce stared down at the picture. He was right. It had indeed.

"Yeah," she said softly. "I liked it too."

Arriving home from work early on Friday, Joyce carried her small shopping bag into the bedroom and knelt to pull the storage boxes out from under the bed. The one she was looking for was toward the middle, requiring the extraction of the more accessible ones in front to reach it.

Flipping the lid off the box she was looking for, she snorted at the few miniskirts and other paraphernalia she'd kept from a time in her life she'd almost forgotten about. They seemed so ridiculously out of place in her life now. She didn't even know why she'd kept them. There were just a few things she hadn't wanted to part with and thought might be handy for Halloween or something sometime.

It hadn't lasted very long, but she had gone through a bit of a goth phase during her later teenage years. In addition to the purple hair, fishnets, spiderweb tights, patent-leather six-inch platform boots, striped wristbands and approximately a complete pencil of black eyeliner per week had all been part of the picture. She'd had no idea Pete would have any interest in it, so she had never mentioned it to him.

She found the item she was looking for and shook it out. The crunched-up vinyl made a snapping sound as it creaked apart. She set the miniskirt on the bed and smoothed it. The silver zipper that ran the entire length of the front had dulled a bit with time.

She stared at it and was startled by the visceral memory the garment elicited—like a song, or a smell. Instantaneously she was launched back to her Floridian studio apartment and the achingly long nights on her feet in a hot, loud, crowded bar. She'd sometimes found it fun at the time, which was hard for her to imagine now.

She reached for the box and lifted out what had been one of her favorite corsets. The center and back panels were black vinyl, joined by a pattern of horizontal black-and-white stripes on the sides. Three chunky silver buckles ran up the center.

Shedding her blouse and slacks, Joyce wrapped the skirt around her waist and zipped it up. A little more snug than she remembered, but it still fit. Maneuvering her hands under it, she grasped at her panties and pulled them off. That particular skirt had never gotten along with underclothes. She wound the corset around her torso and struggled to get the side zipper all the way up. When she was finally into it, she fluffed her cleavage and pulled out her black-and-white-striped wristbands.

How funny that she and Pete had been married three years and had never known of this commonality between them. Joyce reached back into the box and, one by one, pulled out the black, knee-high, lace-up boots. She looked at them warily.

At one time, she had known how to walk in them. Gingerly she lowered her foot into one and zipped it up. She repeated with the other foot, and after adjusting the laces, stood. She was surprised by how natural they felt—appearances aside, their familiarity was unquestionable.

Joyce picked up the bag from Spencer's Gifts. She hadn't entered a Spencer's in years, and being in there had reminded her why. The only patron there that appeared older than twenty-two, she had maneuvered her way through the tight aisles to the back wall and been relieved to see that it was close enough to Halloween for the wigs to be in stock.

She pulled her shiny new costume accessory now from its see-through bag. The style wasn't the same: it was thicker than her hair and had a dense fringe of bangs. But the shade of royal purple was almost identical.

Joyce carried it into the bathroom and brushed it out. It really was a beautiful color. For just a moment she missed wearing it every day, and she smiled at her silliness. Twisting her fair hair up and pinning it as flat as she could against her head, she lifted the wig and carefully maneuvered it over her scalp. Then she began to meticulously outline her eyes in a way she hadn't for more than a decade, smearing jet-black around her eyelids until her eyes somehow gave the impression of a pouty glare regardless of her actual expression. She slathered black mascara over her upper and lower lashes and had to rummage through her makeup drawer quite a bit to locate a tube of blood-red lipstick.

When she was done, she turned to look at herself in the full-length mirror. Her immediate response was to laugh. Head to toe in gleaming black, reams of shining purple polyester framed her face, the bangs almost reaching her eyelashes as her heavily outlined green eyes blinked back at her. Her lips were the color of ripe cherries.

Wow, I used to look this way all the time on purpose, she thought as she left the bathroom. She made her way down to the basement—carefully, given the six-inch platform heels—and pulled the photo from the top of the box.

She was smiling; she did look happy in the picture. The assertion of Joyce's perceived independence hadn't come with just a hair-color change, though Pete was right: it had represented something for her. Her parents never stopped forbidding her to dye her hair, but she had been well aware that their orders and prohibitions would see a hard and immediate end when she turned eighteen. That was the age at which, by law, they didn't get to tell her what to do anymore.

It was one she'd looked forward to for years.

By the end of the summer the picture was taken, Joyce was a couple thousand miles away from the home and family with which she'd grown up. She'd taken off and found refuge on the western coast of Florida, eschewing college and falling into making her living as a bartender in the warmth of the state's coastal sun.

Years later, she would go to college because she wanted to, not because she was told she had to.

Joyce looked at the picture, searching for what her husband had seen. Searching for who she'd been back then. Was it different from who she was now?

Of course, life had been different then. She hadn't understood yet what it meant to live on one's own, support oneself financially, do things her parents, however great their ideological differences, had always taken care of for her. Joyce didn't feel, however, that the rebelliousness she'd exhibited and felt so strongly was naive or without worth. Far from it. What she'd done then had been important.

She looked into the beaming gaze staring back at her. Then she saw it. She saw what her husband had seen when he looked into the same eyes.

It was joy. Pure, simple joy.

She heard Pete come home and tossed the picture back into the box. Lurching toward the stairs, she made her way up them as fast as she could and paused to compose herself at the top. Then she started toward the kitchen where she heard her husband stirring.

PVC creaked as she walked through the house. An involuntary smile lifted her lips; she had forgotten what dressing like this felt like. Her body felt like a pillar, strong and straight, encapsulated snugly in the corset, miniskirt and boots. The purple wig swished as she strode forward.

Pete did a double take when he saw her. The mail in his hand hung limp as he stared.

It had been a long time since Pete had looked at her like that, since she'd had that kind of effect on him. Joyce was surprised by the rush of arousal that lit up her system. She watched her husband's eyes as they traveled slowly up and down her body, his lips parted in surprise.

He finished and met her gaze again but appeared at a loss for words. Joyce smiled, and a soft "Wow" finally emerged from his lips.

"Ready to go?" she asked as she stepped forward and linked her arm through his.

"Where?" he managed to get out, showing no inclination to move.

She laughed. "Somewhere we can cause trouble." She winked and pulled him toward the garage door through which he'd just come.

Pete, still staring, didn't answer, and she turned and bent over to pick up her purse. She heard him swallow.

"I don't know what to wear," he said finally, his eyes still on her outfit.

"You wear that," she said, grabbing her coat as she pulled him out the door.

She wound the three-quarter-length trench coat around herself and tied the belt before climbing into the car. As her husband settled into the driver's seat, she noticed the bulge in his pants. He was hard. The revelation took her breath away a little, and the heat she'd felt since he'd caught sight of her surged through her system. She supposed she could have expected it, but she didn't know the last time Pete had gotten hard just looking at her.

"Where do you want to go?"

Where did she want to go? The idea of actually going to a bar, as she would have wanted to back then, brought a slight grimace to her face. She considered. Then her eyes lit up. She bit her lip, sending Pete a shy sidelong glance. "How about McKinsey's?"

Pete's eyebrows raised. "The hotel?"

Joyce batted her eyelashes a bit and smiled innocently at him. "They have a nice bar there. We could have a drink."

Pete's eyes ran up and down her again in the dark. "Yeah. A drink." He shook himself and started the car. "Works for me."

When they pulled up outside the upscale hotel, a valet opened Joyce's door, and she arranged her coat carefully as she stepped out. Pete walked around to meet her, and it occurred to her that he seemed literally unable to take his eyes off her. Excitement fluttered low in her stomach.

"We're going to skip the drink," Pete murmured as they

stepped into the high-ceilinged lobby. Joyce looked at him, secretly thrilled, as he slanted a smile down at her and led them toward the counter that ran along one side of the elegant room. The entrance to the bar was on the other side.

It took a moment for her to realize the sound level had fallen when they'd walked in. Joyce looked around to see a number of people not even hiding the fact that they were staring, and she blushed as she realized she'd been so caught up in her plan that she'd forgotten the kind of reaction her outfit might bring in public. Everyone around her didn't know she was just playing a fun little game with her husband.

Pete showed no sign of disturbance at the stares, and Joyce felt a wave of warmth. If someone had asked her yesterday how she thought her husband might respond to being blatantly stared at and judged by throngs of strangers because of something regarding her, she would have said she wasn't sure. That he was not embarrassed—or at least hid it very well—brought forth a wave of gratitude with a strength that surprised her.

She used to not care either, back when she'd dressed like this regularly. Of course, most people then hadn't seemed to—as she recalled, most of the inhabitants of the Florida metropolis where she'd lived hadn't blinked at an eighteen-year-old walking around with bright-purple hair and wearing vinyl from head to toe.

This northeastern crowd seemed to expect more from a thirtysomething woman on the arm of a man in a business suit. Joyce looked up at Pete, and his smile was calm as he met her eyes. She pressed closer to his body as they arrived at the counter. Pete requested a room from the woman behind it.

Joyce met the receptionist's eyes and at first shrugged off the fact that the woman didn't smile back. As she took Pete's credit card information and explained the policies to him in a tight voice, the reason for the cool reception finally dawned on Joyce.

She thinks he's paying me.

The receptionist finished with the transaction and handed Pete their key cards. Joyce was still looking at her, and the woman made eye contact one more time and actually glared at her, clearing her throat pointedly before turning away to reach for the phone. Joyce stood still, shocked by the recognition she'd just undergone but even more shocked by the woman's demeanor. What if he were paying her? Would it be that much of a reason to dispose of all customs of politeness and customer service?

Pete put his arm around her, and Joyce clacked with him across the shiny floor to the elevators. The sound level in the lobby had gradually risen, though Joyce didn't doubt at this point that some of the voices they heard were murmuring about them. What a very odd society they lived in. Was it that big of a deal if someone wanted to dress differently from the standard nine-to-five cookie-cutter bullshit in this city? As for the whore perception, who gave a shit if she was taking Pete upstairs to fuck him for money? What business was it of theirs?

Joyce felt a slither of the rebellious anger she'd experienced almost constantly in her teenage years. The familiarity was noticeable even as it was tempered—or perhaps complemented—by the fifteen years of life she'd lived between then and now. She was surprised to realize she hadn't felt that energy for a long time. It added something—potency? passion?—to her immediate experience as they reached the elevator bank. It was what made her untie her coat and shrug out of it as they stood waiting for one to arrive. Calmly she folded her coat over one arm, unsure if the noise level had just lowered a notch again or if it was only her imagination.

An elevator arrived, and they stepped into it. They were alone.

"Jeez, I forgot the kind of reaction wearing this in public

might get." Joyce did her best to keep her voice light as the doors closed behind them.

Pete chuckled. "It would be nice to think people had better things to do than worry about what other people are wearing," he agreed, his eyes on the numbers above the door as they beeped with each ascension.

Joyce smiled and moved to hold his hand. He stiffened slightly, and she stopped. "What's the matter?" For a second she feared the public's reaction had reached her husband, that he was suddenly looking at her like they had. "Are you embarrassed to be seen with me?" She blurted the words before she could stop herself.

Pete's chuckle turned to a guffaw. With another glance at the numbers, he turned fully toward her, and Joyce felt the heat emanating from his body as he seemed to move closer without taking a step. Joyce fell back a pace at the influx of intensity.

"No, I'm not embarrassed to be seen with you. I'm a little jumpy because you look so fucking hot that I feel like a teenager about to blow a load in my pants just looking at you, and I want to fuck you up against the wall of this elevator right now. Feeling any part of you touch any part of me isn't helping the restraint it's taking not to do that. So what anybody downstairs thought about you or me or the stock market in Asia is just about the farthest thing from my mind right now."

Joyce's jaw dropped. She had never heard Pete talk quite that way before—nor had she heard the tone of voice with which he had said it. The energy she'd felt in the lobby came flooding back—a mix of arousal, self-possession, power and freedom. It was a way she was unused to feeling in the last decade, and for a second she was almost light-headed.

The elevator dinged as it halted. Pete grabbed her waist and pulled her close, but just as he seemed about to kiss her, he turned her roughly around and nudged her through the doors, his long strides behind her as they walked down the hall single file. Apparently she wasn't moving quite fast enough for him, because a second later Pete had stopped and scooped her up in his arms, eliciting a gasp of surprise from Joyce, who was aware that anyone they met in the hall now was going to get a clear look of just how few undergarments she had on.

As they reached their door, Pete maneuvered his arm to hand her the key cards he'd been carrying. Joyce pulled one out of the small envelope and slid it into the metal door handle. When the little light turned green, she pulled down on the handle, and Pete shoved the door wide open with one foot.

Somehow it wasn't until that moment that Joyce realized she was breathless, that she had been since the elevator and that she was all but panting now as her body reminded her she needed to breathe. At the same time she became acutely aware of the swelling in her clit and how much she wanted her husband—any part of him—to touch her there. Now.

She was surprised when Pete set her on her feet at the foot of the bed rather than directly on it. Before she could question the move, he launched himself at her and she fell backward onto it anyway, startled—though by this time not surprised—by her husband's urgent carnality. He grabbed her knees and spread her legs, looking at her naked flesh beneath the miniskirt, which had ridden up to her hips without any coaxing. Joyce could feel her wetness as her husband stared at her, and suddenly her impatience matched his.

"Fuck me," she whispered. The purple wig tickled her jawline, but she quickly stopped noticing as Pete struggled out of his pants and crawled back on top of her, his hard cock positioned at the slippery entrance to her pussy. She could feel the tension in his body as he held back, and knowing the effect she was having on him made a rush of arousal spill onto his waiting cock.

Pete sucked in a breath. "I need to be in you now, baby," he panted in her ear. "And I'm going to come fast. Is that okay?"

Joyce was already undulating her hips desperately trying to coax him inside her. She would have thought that would be a sufficient answer, but since he seemed to be waiting for one, she hissed out an urgent "Yes," as she spread her legs wider beneath him.

Pete plummeted into her, and she cried out, meeting his thrusts as he fucked her harder, faster, deeper. His hand snaked up and twisted into the purple strands against her cheek, and the way he grunted made her not even mind that he wasn't actually pulling her hair. Though not as satisfying as a true tug on her blonde locks, it was obviously having an effect on him, and it was one with which she wasn't about to argue.

Joyce's core felt a constant jolt of arousal as Pete hammered into her, the feeling of taking her husband's cock more satisfying than it had felt for a long time. His strangled cry indicating that he couldn't hold back anymore almost pushed Joyce over the edge, and she gripped his body with her legs as he came deep inside her. She squeezed him tight, reveling in the power she had to affect him that way.

Breathing heavily, he pulled out and rolled over onto his back, reaching for her immediately. He grabbed her waist and pulled her on top of him so she was straddling his torso.

"I'm sorry," he panted.

"Why?"

"Because I didn't let you come first, of course. That's against the rules, isn't it?" He winked even as his hand slid forward to meet the sheen of sweat and arousal that graced her inner thigh.

"Fuck the rules," she said—and meant it.

She'd looked the way she had in that picture because she had done something she wanted—and had felt, for once, that she truly had the freedom to. The arbitrary orders of someone else didn't apply to her anymore.

That novelty had worn off, it seemed, without her even noticing it. She'd been back in the world of rules now for more than a decade, and she'd forgotten what it felt like to know something she wanted and own the freedom to follow it, to remember she wasn't indebted to somebody's arbitrary rules telling her she couldn't have it. Like wearing vinyl and purple hair into one of the most upscale hotels in the area. Or loving the feeling of her husband's cock in her so much she didn't even care that she hadn't had an orgasm yet. Or, she felt on behalf of all who did, getting paid to fuck if that's what she chose to do.

Pete looked in her eyes, and Joyce's grin was involuntary. For a moment neither of them moved, and even if she hadn't seen the recognition in her husband's face, she knew her eyes looked the exact same way they had in the picture that was the reason they were there. For the first time in a long while, she felt it again. It was exhilarating.

She shrieked in surprise as Pete grasped her waist and pulled her forward, the urgency in his forearms not relaxing until she was straddling his face. Before she could catch her breath, she felt the warmth of his tongue connect with her clit. A low moan broke from her throat, and the tremor that started in her body was electrified by the energy that felt like it was embracing her every cell.

It was joy. Pure, simple joy.

MORE LIGHT

Laila Blake

Broken glass crunches under my feet, however carefully I try to move. I remembered to wear heavy boots; I'm not worried about getting hurt, but disturbing the silence in this place seems like a crime in itself. Like shouting in a church or jumping on a tomb. I almost want to hold my breath—first impressions are important. I look around, follow gilded stucco pillars up to a high, decorated ceiling. It might have borne a mural once, but all it has to show now is the natural water-painting of mold and stains, of moisture leaking through the visible cracks. It is eerily beautiful, and instinctively, I raise my camera but the lens is wrong. I need something far more light sensitive. Instead, I imagine the fabulous parties thrown here once upon a time; I see flapper dresses and thighs, energetic dancing, twinkling lights, and a small brass orchestra. In one of the dark corners, a couple could have stood, catching their breath, hands gliding under fabric. A shiver runs down my spine, and I am back to seeing dust and ruins.

Some shafts of sunlight manage to fall through the shattered windows; where the glass remains, though, the milky-gray grime of too many years shields against them all too effectively. I snap a picture of the infinitesimal dust particles glinting there, smile and follow the shaft of light through the viewfinder.

"You need these?" George calls from behind me. I jump at the volume and turn around. He was being manly, herding me away from the trunk so that he could carry in the equipment. Now, he is struggling to balance two lighting tripods.

"Definitely later," I say, nodding with a vague motion at the dim interior. "And the softbox and the reflectors," I add with a sheepish grin. I take the tripods off him and store them in a less photogenic corner, then I reach for the light meter in my bag and start to walk around the room again. His shouting seems to have shattered something and the atmosphere feels less sacred, less stifling. There is dust and crumbled debris everywhere.

George is the more finicky of the two of us—although, by long tradition, he would say that I am just messy. When he comes back, he carries a foldout table for the equipment, gives me a look and picks my bag up from the floor. He dusts it off and puts it on the table. I poke my tongue out at him and push middle and ring finger under my thumb in the universal rock-and-roll sign. He sighs, shakes his head and leaves for more stuff.

We were in college together. Back then, we just happened to hang with the same group of people—photography is impossible to do on your own. He was the handsome, jock type although he never played sports; he just looked like that with his tall physique and his naturally broad shoulders, the wavy dirty-blond hair. He still does. I was the chubby, nerdy one with the glasses and the shy, quiet voice, which I tried to make authoritatively deep. We weren't close but somehow we both ended up in Boston after college. His studio is just ten minutes away from mine and it's good to have friends who get it, friends who actually enjoy spending an hour driving around Connecticut to sneak into a long-abandoned building. Neither of us can afford an assistant.

I can hear him pottering around with the equipment behind me, but I'm still walking around, looking at the walls in the different rooms. From time to time, a little bit of dust falls from the ceiling and my heart beats a little faster. I try to be more graceful.

"First impression?" George asks coming up behind me. Less body conscious, he touches everything, hangs against the moldy doorjamb in a way I would never dare.

"There's something here," I say slowly and shrug. We both know that we've been to more impressively abandoned places, but this one has a solemn quality all its own that will be difficult to catch on camera. George hums in assent and we start to walk around, to try and find these special spots in which the natural light provides enough eerie illumination. Too much artificial light would ruin it, I think. I stroll back to the table and exchange my lens for a more light-sensitive one. It lies heavy in my hand and I almost drop it when I hear a loud crunching, dragging sound from somewhere in the bowels of the building. Just for a moment, I am sure this is when the zombies finally attack, but then I come back to reality, screw the lens on my camera and go to investigate.

George is dragging something over the floor, with a sound like a hundred tiny bells, and when he emerges from the shadow I see his broad grin and the ancient chandelier he's dug up from somewhere. It is dusty and broken in many places but it's still gorgeous, some herald of older times.

"Wow," I say—if just because it makes him grin with self-satisfaction as he gently drapes it into a shaft of sunlight.

We start shooting, find the best angle, the one that contrasts glittering light against squalor. My heart is beating faster; finally something is coming together.

If I wasn't used to George, he would be distracting to the point of annoyance. As it is, I smile and let him get on with his athleticism. I have long found that George just enjoys using his body—it makes him feel better about his photos. He crouches on the floor, then lies down completely, moving over the debris like a war-zone journalist through the sand. I am more stationary; I squat in place, fumble with the controls, find the perfect aperture settings. I am more given to placing the camera on the floor and snapping away with a remote than performing acrobatics. But I find myself momentarily entranced. From my vantage point, he is half hidden by the sparkling bits of polished glass and he stares at them with such a concentrated intensity, I just have to take a picture. He doesn't resist. Years of training and spending time with other photographers have ground photo shyness out of both of us. I find a different angle and click again, check the image on the screen. It is a beautiful portrait. I feel that rarely reoccurring flash of affection, the memory of a long-abandoned crush. When I let the camera sink, he smiles at me and returns the gesture, click, my thoughtful, aching face. I have that sudden childish urge to throw my hands in front of my face and launch myself in his direction to grab the camera and delete all evidence, but I stay there, squatting, hugging my knees for balance.

I give him a half smile instead and raise my camera. We regard each other through the viewfinders, only seeing shiny black surfaces where eyes and nose should be. Photography robots. The two clicks are almost simultaneous. Just like back in college.

"You know what would make this better?" he asks, carefully raising himself from the ground, mindful of the expensive equipment in his hand. I raise my brows, encourage him to go on.

"Nudity."

I snort and roll my eyes.

"Right, because the only real contribution women can make to photography is to take their clothes off..."

George just grins, above me now, my face at the level of his crotch, and he touches the tip of my nose. Just for a moment I want to be a different me, in a different body, and go right ahead. But then he shakes his head.

"You and your assumptions," he chides with that naughty schoolboy grin on his face. "Who said I was talking about you?"

My mouth falls open, just for a second, and my eyebrows seem intent on trying to disappear under my hairline. George laughs and offers me a hand to pull myself up from the floor. I accept. His hand is warm and I bite at the side of my lip, feeling lumpy in my long, shapeless sweater-dress and tights I'm wearing for comfort of movements.

"It would make good pictures," I agree, frowning as professionally as I can at the scenery. George seems satisfied. He hands me his camera and pulls his sweater over his head. It is a careless gesture only people with beautiful bodies, people without shame could be capable of. I place the strap of his camera around my neck and raise my own. In the first picture, he is unbuttoning his jeans; in the next he has pushed them to his knees. I snap the next of the curve of his back. In the shaft of lights, the tiny knobs of his spine are visible though his sleeveless shirt.

"I've always liked your portrait work," he says casually when he has finally liberated his jeans from his sneakers. My heart beats faster and I grin, not even capable of waving the compliment away.

"Thanks," I manage, and I catch that glimpse of stomach in the sun as he is pulling up his shirt. There is a fine light-brown line of hair that runs down into his tight boxer-briefs. It is just a shade darker than his hair. I exhale a shallow breath; send a prayer to the god of professionalism. But then he meets my eyes and he holds my gaze, fierce and serious in a way I have hardly ever seen him. I know he's pulling down his boxers but my eyes are arrested, held in place. Almost in panic, I throw my camera between us and manage a picture of that expression before it fades.

He doesn't cover himself; I wet my bottom lip and wordlessly direct him into the light. It throws beautifully stark shadows over his chest and face: planes of light and dark, all angles and masculinity only the magic of light and shadow can create. When I finally dare a glance at his crotch, I hardly manage to take it in before I tear my eyes away. He is not aroused—but I am. Tingling and nervous.

He looks like a god in the tiny preview screen. I ask him to pick up the chandelier and hold it up next to him: a hundred lights sparkle over his chest. I want to render these in black and white, I think—time in the studio will tell. I click, click, click—I can't get enough of the lights, of his body, his face. For long moments I get so lost in the work, I almost forget the aching tingly feeling between my legs but it always comes back, harder and more demanding than before.

Finally, I hand him back his camera, and he raises his brows questioningly as he sets the chandelier back onto the floor and shakes out his arm, tired from holding it up too long.

"Vulnerable photographer in dark corners," I tell him with a smile and bring a tripod, light and soft-box from the table.

"Still trying to be deep," he teases, and I want to blush, but I think I manage not to.

"Trying to be?" I ask instead, jokingly menacing where I don't feel like either. Not deep down. But he just looks at me for a moment too long and then starts to take pictures. He keeps the camera just far enough from his face to let me capture his expression, his natural body language. He is beautiful and I find myself envying his freedom. I catch him squatting by the chandelier, checking his setting, staring almost meditatively at the view-screen.

"Aren't you cold?" I finally ask. I never know how long I'm snapping away, but I finally caught a close-up of his shoulder and arm and I saw the gooseflesh rising there.

"Not very," he answers, but I think he's lying. I let my camera sink and take a deep breath. George is still watching me.

"What?" I finally ask.

He cocks up his chin, just once.

"Your turn."

For the second time, my jaw drops. This time I am more prepared for it. Raising any opposition isn't easy, and I take a deep breath.

"I'm not..." I start, but George interrupts me, before I can denigrate my looks, the state of my hair, or any of the million other imperfections I could name.

"You are," he says with a strange emphasis. "You really are." His eyes travel down my shoulder and along the side of my breast and he finally smiles. And there is something in his smile that has power and magic, especially in a place like this and without clothes to detract from his magnetism. I finally shrug as though I, too, think nothing of it. As though I do this all the time. I hand him my camera and try not to linger too long with my hands clinging to the hem of my long sweater.

"There'll be pressure marks all over," I warn ahead, then open my mouth again to say something else, something about my thighs or my stomach but then I don't.

"They'll plush out soon enough," he assures me, and I turn

around to pull the sweater over my face. I suck a sharp breath through my teeth at the cold against my skin. With my shoes, I clear a patch of ground and kick them off. Then I peel down my tights, my panties and finally reach back to open my bra. Unlike me, George grants me that moment of privacy. He is fumbling with the light and his settings. When he concentrates like this, a strand of hair falls into his face. His frown and the stance of his naked body suddenly take away from his jock appeal—he seems buffer in clothes but more handsome without them; he looks thoughtful and somehow *more*, deeper. I feel my chest flutter.

"Ready?" he asks, looking up at me. He comes around and picks my clothes up, then moves them out of frame. Out of reach. Wearing his sneakers but still nothing else, I notice that his cock is not quite as disinterested in the proceedings anymore, perking up as though in greeting. I feel more naked immediately and tear my eyes away, but also less nervous.

"Ready."

"Good, move against the window." His voice changes when he takes pictures. I have noticed that before. He is serious and intense. "Like that, look outside; place your hands on the window, careful where it's broken."

I try to take deep breaths; he tells me to relax and I do my best. Muscle by muscle I force the tension to flow out of my body.

"Ass too," he finally chides with a grin in his voice, and I have to laugh.

"Fuck you," I say, giggling, shake myself, and when I return to position he hums in assent. I can hear the camera shutter click and click. So fast, furiously clicking at every inch of my naked skin, the plush curve of my hip where it moves into the narrower waist. I turn toward him only a few degrees to let him catch just the hint of my breast. During those first poses, I feel torn between being all too conscious of my body, the extra softness, the lines and dimples over my ass—and my professional knowledge of taking pictures of women's bodies, and how to make them all believe in their own style of beauty. With time, I start to gravitate toward the latter. Moving slowly, I stretch myself, turn around and lean against the wall—grappling for courage I stare down the lens. A storm of clicks washes over me. The fear is starting to fade to exhilaration, adrenaline. We try more adventurous poses; I crouch in the dirt behind the chandelier, I rise up high to my toes, I turn around and touch my ass, my breasts. I place my chin on my shoulder and run my hands through my hair. I feel like one sore nerve ending, ready to explode at the smallest touch. Every once in a while he issues demands but for the most part, he seems happy to go along with my sudden sense of freedom.

When I take a break to stretch my arms out and rub them against the cold, George mounts his camera on a tripod, carefully sets the field and then nods at me to turn toward the wall. I hear the shutter click again, and again, and suddenly his hands encircle my waist. Another click—I hold my breath.

"You are beautiful," he whispers against my hair. *Click.* His teeth graze over my neck and I feel his cock pushing up against my ass. *Click, click.* Then he turns me around, and there is something in his eyes—seeking, wanting. I know that feeling, and for a moment seeing it in his eyes hits me like a slap across the face of an unconscious person. I wake up gasping for air and lean in to kiss him. He crosses the rest of the distance. *Click.* *Click.* I find the remote in his hand and take it from him; I can hardly breathe. His hands run down my arms and up my waist until his thumbs caress the undersides of my breasts. This time I release the shutter: *click. Click.* He walks me back a step; I find myself pressed against the wall, cool against my ass; then his hand is between my legs and my head falls back. *Click, moan, click.* With two fingers inside of me, the world grows hazier, I hardly think of the photos anymore, just know that the click sends tiny shoots of electricity through my body. I kiss his chest, his shoulders—he is so hard and tight under his skin, no softness like my body has in abundance. *Click.* Curling his fingers, he touches that perfect point inside me and I rise to my toes, aching, breathing, moaning. My tongue travels up his sternum; he tastes like salt and I want more. Soon I can't keep quiet and he lifts my leg over his hip. The angle is terrible but god, his cock feels good against my clit. *Click. Click.*

"A... around. Turn me around again," I moan, and his lips crash onto mine, hands grappling my face hard once more before he pushes me against the wall. My fingers find purchase, and I spread my legs. I can hear his aching sigh and suddenly, his hands push my ass apart and his tongue takes one long drag all the way from my clit up my crack. Fuck, fuck! He is fucking me with his tongue; I go cross-eyed for long heartbeats at a time and the grimy wall in front of me fades in and out of focus. A moment later he is inside of me. So full, so tight. His hand lands next to mine on the wall, and our fingers cross. We groan in unison, and he pushes his teeth into my neck. I almost forget: *click, click, click, click.*

The wall under my fingers is rough and he is digging his hand into my hip so hard it almost hurts, pushing into me again and again. With each thrust it feels like he's pressing every atom of air in my lungs, and each time I have to moan to let it out, or I might burst. And still I want more, more.

Slipping my hand between my legs, I find my clit and he sounds another groan. I return the remote; I need my hand to keep myself upright against the wall. Immediately the clicks storm faster, more aggressively; he seems to time two with each thrust: I am curled inward, rubbing, panting, greedy.

"I want you to come all over my cock," he breathes hot against my ear and I could cry it sounds so good. My body grants his wish less than a minute later, rearing, crying out and contracting all around him. He curses, groans and then pulls out. The splatter of his come lands on my ass and he whines like a wounded creature and collapses against my back. I shiver, find his hands and pull them more tightly around me.

"Hi," I whisper. It still sounds frighteningly loud in the silence. George moves his head, his lips brush against my shoulder and finally, he turns me around again. I hardly dare to look—but he's smiling.

"You're cold." His fingers trace my arms, then he rubs them a little ineffectually. We both feel gelatinous and tired.

"I didn't notice," I say, and grin. So does he. *Click.* We kiss. *Click, click.* He tastes even better now.

"Let's pack up... I want to get you somewhere warm. Somewhere with a bed."

I don't know what to say but I curl my arms around him; his hands find my ass again, smearing his come, and pull me against him. *Click.* Somewhere warm with a bed is exactly what we need.

STAY WITH ME

Crystal Jordan

Damn, it was hot. The roasting heat of the Texas day had spilled over into a sweltering night. A languid breeze barely made the curtains ruffle, and a sheen of sweat coated Jamie's body. She stared at the ceiling, too hot and restless to sleep. Annoyed, she kicked the twisted sheet away and heaved herself out of bed. Shoving open the French doors, she stepped out onto the porch that wrapped around the house.

A few lights shone from the barns and she heard the occasional neigh of a horse, but the rest of the ranch seemed to have managed the slumber that eluded her. Twelve years of living in the middle of nowhere and, though she cherished the quiet, she'd never quite adjusted to the summer humidity. Sighing, she leaned against the railing.

"Can't sleep?"

The low voice brought her upright. "Cord."

His boots crunched in the gravel before he climbed the three steps onto the porch. Her heart fluttered the way it always did when he was around, and it was all she could do not to fall back a step as he came near. She tried for a light tone. "The heat's keeping you up too, huh?"

"No." He moved a little closer, into her personal space, and her pulse sped. She was suddenly very aware of the fact that she wore nothing underneath her cotton nightgown.

Her nipples tightened, pushing against the thin material, and she had to resist the urge to cross her arms. "No? Then what's got you up at two in the morning?"

"You."

His dark gaze zeroed in on her chest, and she saw a flicker of pure lust in his expression. An answering throb of desire settled low in her belly. The night closed in around them, making it feel like they were the only two people in the world. Being alone with this man was a dangerous temptation. He took another step toward her and she skittered back until the doorjamb pressed between her shoulder blades. He loomed over her, huge and masculine and far too sexy. "Invite me in, Jamie."

Her hormones clamored an emphatic agreement at that suggestion, but she shook her head. "I'm your boss. That would be a bad idea."

Nothing could keep the quaver of longing out of her voice, though. Liquid flames licked at her core at the very thought of inviting Cord Preston into her bedroom. She tried to squelch the need and failed. As usual. She'd been unable to control the way her body responded to him since she'd hired him as a horse trainer three months before. She'd been worse than a lovesick teenager, hanging out in the barns to talk to him for hours—about anything and everything. Even then, she'd resisted acting on this insane attraction. He'd hired on for the season, and then he'd be gone. Temporary sexual arrangements weren't her style.

He leaned forward until his lips were no more than a hairs-breadth from hers. "It's too late for either of us to stop this thing, sweetheart, and I'm tired of pretending we don't want each other. Invite me in." It was more demand than request, and his hot breath rushed over her skin as he spoke. "I'm dying to be inside you, Jamie."

Cord. Inside her. Her sex clenched, and it took every ounce of her willpower not to arch into his body and finally, *finally* know what it was like to have his hands on her flesh.

His voice dropped to a coaxing rumble. "I need to touch you. Let me."

"Yes," she whispered, the word spilling out before she could stop it.

The tips of his fingers grazed her thigh where her nightshirt ended, and goose bumps broke on her limbs. She felt the light rasp of his calluses, and her knees quivered.

"Inside, sugar." Urging her into the bedroom, he shut the door behind them. Hearing the lock snick into place made this all too real, and she put a bit of space between them, trying to catch her breath.

He grabbed the bottom of his T-shirt and pulled it over his head. Tossing it aside, he said, "Now you."

She shouldn't do it. Nothing had really happened yet. She could call this off right now. Instead, she gathered up the folds of her gown and stripped. The flare of hunger in his gaze made lava flow through her veins, melting her resistance. It might be stupid and wrong, but just this once, she was going to give in.

A hot blush suffused her cheeks when his dark gaze roamed over her naked body. The heat spread downward until every inch of her skin felt flushed and sensitized. That he still wore jeans only emphasized her own nudity. His broad chest was bare, sprinkled with springy-looking curls. Her heart pounded, blood rushing through her veins.

A discarded coil of braided leather rope sat on her dresser and he reached over to pick it up. Glancing up to meet her eyes, he flashed a tiny, wicked smile. "Let's make this interesting."

"Interesting?" She swallowed. Her legs shook so badly she had to sit on the edge of the mattress. "I don't know—"

"I do." He captured first one ankle and then the other and bound each to the footboard, spreading her like a feast on her own bed. "Trust me?"

She nodded.

This was something she'd never tried before, but the nervousness she expected to feel never surfaced. Deep down, she knew Cord would never hurt her. So when he finished securing her arms straight over her head with his belt, anticipation arced through her like lightning in a gathering storm.

He shifted around until he knelt between her legs, his gaze lingering on her breasts and exposed sex. She bit back a moan, her nipples beaded and wetness coated the folds of her pussy. The way he grinned and licked his lips told her he noticed every detail of her reaction.

"You have no idea how long I've wanted this." His hands pressed her thighs even wider, his iron grip unyielding. She shuddered, her need winding so taut she thought she might snap. He groaned, shook his head. "I can't wait another minute."

Then he buried his face between her legs, and she arched, a thin scream breaking from her throat. Heat exploded through her, burning like a wildfire. His mouth formed around her clit, his tongue sweeping over the tight bundle of nerves until she writhed and sobbed. Pleasure coiled within her with a swiftness that shocked her. It only took seconds for him to have her on the edge of breaking. She wanted to drive her hands into his hair and hold him closer until she exploded. More. That was all she wanted, all she could think about. *More.*

She shouldn't want this, shouldn't like it so much. But her husband had died four years ago, and there had been no one since then. After the worst of her grief had passed, the lonely nights had been the hardest to endure. She was so hungry for a man's touch, for the weight of him pressing down on top of her. But no one had really tempted her since Travis. Except Cord.

When his fingers teased the lips of her pussy, then thrust into her sex, the sudden penetration had her torso bowing upward. The rope snapped taut, keeping her exactly where Cord wanted her. He chuckled against her swollen flesh, and the vibration made her gasp. Fire streaked down her skin, and every time he pushed his fingers inside her, her inner muscles clenched tight.

"Cord, please!"

He took her clit between his teeth, biting down lightly. She twisted against the bindings, their restriction only making her burn hotter, and a ragged cry ripped from her throat. His hand angled until he rubbed her in just the right spot, and she slammed over into orgasm so fast that stars burst behind her eyes.

"I forgot…"

She blinked slowly as the world came back into focus. "Forgot, what?"

"This." He moved up her body until his mouth could cover hers, and she tasted herself on his lips. It made her whimper with a renewed surge of desire. He licked his way into her mouth, sucking on her bottom lip, nipping at the soft flesh just enough to make her jerk. One big palm covered her breast, his fingers pinching and rolling her nipple. It was exquisite agony, sharpening her longing into white-hot need.

He reared back, breaking the kiss as he jerked open the fly on his jeans. It took him only a moment to sheathe his long cock in a condom. His eyes glittered with lust, a flush running under his deep tan. He braced himself on his elbows over her. "I'm going to ride you hard, Jamie."

"Yes." Oh, yes. She wanted him inside her, had craved it since the day she'd met him, no matter how she'd denied it. But there was no more fooling herself. Cord had stripped away any pretense tonight.

The head of his cock nudged at her opening, and she pulled against the rope to get closer. He sank into her one slow inch at a time, and the stretch was divine. He shuddered when he was hilted in her pussy, a hiss escaping from between his clenched teeth.

His throat worked. "You're so damn tight."

"It's...been a while." She bit her lip, wriggled under him, moaned as the curls on his chest stimulated her nipples. "Can you hurry up and move now?"

"God, yes." Then he did exactly as he'd promised—he rode her hard. She strained against the ropes to pump her hips up and meet each downward thrust. He filled her to the limit, and she loved every second.

It was almost rough, the speed and force of their movements slamming the headboard against the wall. The mattress squeaked beneath them, and their groans echoed in the wide bedroom, a carnal symphony that ratcheted up her craving. Sweat slipped down their bodies, the humid air wrapping around them. It had already been too hot tonight, but they'd turned the room steamy. Her pussy fisted around his dick, a precursor to climax. She was so close. The thought alone was enough to make her sex spasm again.

"*Jamie*," he rasped. His thighs shoved hers as wide as the rope would let them go, and his jeans chafed her legs as he pistoned in and out of her, but the small discomfort only seemed to make it better.

He rammed deep and ground his pelvis against her clit. She imploded, her pussy clenching in rhythmic waves, tingles breaking down her limbs. Her mouth opened in a silent scream as he fucked her through her orgasm, forcing her to another peak. One, two, three more thrusts and he froze over her, shuddering and groaning as he came. His forehead dropped to rest against hers, his body shaking.

After a long moment, he reached up and untied her wrists. She shivered as he rubbed the tender skin, kissing her palms one at a time. Moving back on his knees, he unfastened the rope around her ankles. He massaged feeling back into her limbs, and she purred at the almost gentle stroking of his calloused fingertips.

"I'll be right back," he rumbled. Then he disappeared into the bathroom.

She sighed, relaxed in a way that only truly amazing sex could make a woman. Her thoughts drifted, exhaustion sweeping over her.

The mattress dipped as he settled next to her, his arm curving over her hip. It should've been strange to have someone besides Travis in bed with her, holding her. She almost expected to feel a wave of guilt, but she didn't. She'd loved her husband and she missed him, but he was gone and she was a young and healthy woman with needs. What she felt was...good. Satiated in a way she hadn't been in four long years.

A little smile quirked her lips as Cord's fingers drifted in slow circles across her skin. Her breathing slowed and she closed her eyes.

"Sleep," he commanded.

There was no other choice. She went over into unconsciousness, his arms wrapped around her. She wouldn't mind staying this way forever.

It felt as if no time had passed when she rolled over and stretched, her muscles protesting after the hard workout the night before. Turning her head, she found the bed empty. She swallowed and sat up, refusing to give in to the sudden pain that punched through her. Of course, he was gone. He'd gotten what he wanted, hadn't he? All those conversations the last few months didn't mean much in the grand scheme of things. But their talks and those tender moments after they were done with sex just made waking up alone that much more hurtful. If he'd left right away, she wouldn't have expected him to be here now.

Frankly, she shouldn't have expected anything, shouldn't be hurt at all. Sex was sex. She was just rusty on the one-nighter protocol—she hadn't had one since she was nineteen. Still, disappointment pressed down on her chest, and she had to climb out of the bed that smelled of Cord.

He was leaving anyway, she reminded herself fiercely. Only in her lonely, pathetic dreams would a drifter like him ever put down roots. She'd been telling herself that since she'd hired him, but apparently last night had confused her heart and her mind. Well, the stark truth showed its ugly face the morning after, didn't it?

Picking up the nightshirt he'd stripped her out of, she pulled it on and wandered out to the kitchen to make some coffee. Caffeine would make everything a bit better. While the pot percolated, she stepped over to the glass doors that overlooked Ruby Creek Ranch. Dawn was just brightening the sky, streaking it with pinks, yellows and oranges. In a million years, she would never have thought she'd live in a place like this—

acres of rolling hills, with a deep greenness that just sprawled on forever. This should have been the last place that would feel like home, but it did. She loved it here. She'd been a dirt-poor city girl when Travis had brought her here. He'd been attending UCLA and she'd been waiting tables at a diner near campus. A total mismatch, but they'd made it work. She'd come to Texas with him and never looked back.

A few horses trotted in the paddocks by the barn, and she could feel the ranch beginning to stir. The hands would be out tending the livestock soon. After she finished her coffee, she'd go help with the million and one chores it took to keep this operation running. Then she needed to meet with the ranch foreman later in the morning. It would be a busy day, but she found herself lingering.

Boot heels rang on the wooden porch and she straightened. She knew his step well enough to know it was Cord. It was disturbing to realize how aware of him she was. He paused when he came into view, his gaze meeting hers through the door. His hand hovered over the doorknob for a moment, but he didn't grab it. The hesitant gesture after his command in the bedroom last night seemed out of character.

Her eyebrows arched. "Come in."

The door swung inward, and he removed his hat as he entered the room. "Mornin'."

"Good morning." She clasped and unclasped her hands in front of her, hating the way her nerves jangled. "Did you need something?"

The corner of his mouth kicked up in a smile that made her heart flutter. He turned to shut and lock the door behind him. Moving toward her with predatory grace, his dark eyes tracked her every movement as she backed up against the counter. Cornered. Bracing a hand on either side of her, he caged her, towered over her. Her pulse tripped and raced at the heat in his gaze, excitement firing through her system. His grin stretched wider. "Yeah, I need...something."

She made herself stiffen when her body wanted to melt into him. "Good, you can explain the details of that *something* over coffee."

The pot sputtered as if announcing it was done perking. She poked his arm until it dropped, then sidled out from in front of him.

"Are you all right?" The edge of concern in his voice made her heart squeeze.

Ignoring her wayward emotions, she clenched her jaw and pulled two mugs from a cupboard. She decided blunt honesty was the best way to deal with this. "I didn't like waking up alone."

"Ah, damn. Jamie..." His body heat surrounded her as he came up behind her. "I was checking on the mare that just foaled, but I planned to come back, maybe wake you up with a kiss. I'm sorry."

"Don't be sorry." Hunching a shoulder, she didn't turn around. Instead, she reached for the coffee pot and poured hot liquid into their cups. "Last night was..."

"Amazing," he said firmly.

"A mistake." Tightening her mouth, she shifted until she faced him, then pushed one mug into his hand. "I enjoyed it, don't get me wrong. But...I'm not the kind of woman who does short-term flings, Cord. And you're not the kind of man who sticks around. The season's almost over and then you'll be gone."

Nine days until he drove his pickup out of her life. Not that she'd been counting the seconds long before he'd come to her bed.

"Yeah, about that." He squinted down at his coffee, laugh lines digging grooves around his eyes. Lifting the cup to his mouth, he took a sip. "What if I decided not to go?"

Her heart slammed hard against her rib cage, then seized in utter shock. "I don't understand."

"You're still going to need a trainer." His gaze went to the window and the paddocks beyond. "Have you ever thought about expanding?"

She knew she should be keeping up, but the conversation seemed to have tilted into surreal directions. She set aside her coffee, afraid her hands might start trembling so much she'd spill it. "No, Travis was more interested in running cattle than training horses. The horses were Pop's babies. He had the touch, like you."

"You loved him a lot, didn't you?"

She wasn't sure which *him* Cord was talking about, but it didn't really matter. "I loved them both. They were so good to me—it was tough to lose them in the same accident." Truer words had never been spoken, but time had a way of healing, and thinking about them didn't sting as much as it once had. "I'll always miss them."

"I'm sorry you lost them, but I'm glad you had people like that." There was a bleakness to his tone that suggested he *hadn't* had people in his life who cared. It made her want to reach over and hug him.

Maybe she was an idiot, but she did just that. Her arms slipped around his waist, and she pressed her cheek to his chest. After a moment, he wrapped her up in his embrace and held her close.

"I didn't have anyone before I came here. Total orphan, bona fide California city slicker, never had a real home or more than two pennies to rub together." She gave a little laugh. "Pop could have made my life a living hell when his only child showed up with me, two days after we eloped in Vegas. Instead, he welcomed me like a daughter, hugged me tight, said there were some people who spend their lives leaving and some who spend it staying, and I was staying right here at Ruby Creek. And that was that."

Cord caught her chin in his hand, forced her to meet his eyes. "I've spent my whole life leaving, going from one ranch to the next, riding bulls or broncos in the rodeo. After my mom died and my dad bailed...drifting is all I've ever really known." He paused, and she held her breath, hoping he'd continue. He always had plenty to say about horses and ranching, but he'd never been one to talk about himself. She hadn't realized how hungry she'd been to know more about what made him the man he was until now. "I've been thinking...I should be feeling restless, ready to move on. But I'm not. I kept telling myself it's because I like Ruby Creek so well, but that's not the truth. It's because *you're* here."

"Cord, I—"

His grip tightened on her jaw, silencing her. "Once I admitted how much I needed you, I couldn't stay away. But I knew you were wary, and I understood why." Mischief glinted in his gaze. "So, I...forced the issue."

Yeah, that about summed up what he'd done the night before. She snorted.

His expression sobered. "Ask me to stay, Jamie. Tell me you want me here with you."

Pressing her shaking lips together, she swallowed. God, yes, she wanted that. Somehow in the last few months her foolish heart had gone and fallen in love with him. But still, she hesitated. Could she truly handle letting another man into her life, knowing she might lose him too? Was she ready to take that big a risk again?

The pad of his thumb stroked over her chin, and she met his eyes. Understanding shone in the depths of his gaze. That, more than anything, settled her. This man knew her. He made her feel alive after so many years, and that was too precious to let go of easily. If he was willing to stay, she was willing to keep him. It was as simple as that.

"I want you here," she whispered, barely able to squeeze the words past her tight throat. "With me. For as long as you want to stay."

A huge breath whooshed out of him. The smile on his face was brighter and more delighted than any she'd ever seen from him. "Well, then. I think the rest of my life might just be long enough, don't you?"

"Are you sure?" Her fingers bunched in the back of his shirt, hope and disbelief warring within her.

He put his coffee down next to hers, then swung her into his arms and walked toward the bedroom. "Let me show you exactly how sure I am."

"Are you going to actually take your pants off this time?" She tucked her hands behind his neck, stroking through the curls there.

"Absolutely." He nudged the door to her room open. "I have at least a couple of hours before anyone comes looking for me. What about you?"

She tilted her head. "They'll wonder where I am, but no one's going to come knocking until around ten."

"Good, because I intend to take my time."

That was enough to send a wicked shiver coursing through her. Every step he took rubbed her against him and made her body loosen, readying itself for sex. Her nipples thrust against her nightshirt, and she knew he'd notice the moment he put her down.

He laid her on the mattress, his gaze reverent as it moved over her. And, yes, he paused for a split second longer than he needed to on her breasts. "You are so beautiful."

"Thank you. You're pretty good-looking yourself." She flicked her fingers at his clothes. "And I'd like to look at all of you. Now. You got to see me already."

"Yes, I did." He winked, bending over to yank off his boots. Then he straightened to jerk his shirt over his head. She pressed her legs together to savor the ache between them as every tanned inch of him came into view. Heavy pecs sprinkled with hair that trailed down his washboard abs and disappeared below his waistband. He unbuckled his belt and his zipper rasped as he slid it down.

A moan bubbled out of her as he pushed his jeans down and off. His legs were long and muscular, leading up to the impressive arc of his cock. A bead of precum slipped down the thick shaft, and she wanted to catch it with her tongue, suck him hard until he begged her to let him come.

"If you keep looking at me like that, I'm not going to last more than five minutes, sugar." He pulled a condom out of his wallet and tossed it on the bedside table before he set one knee on the mattress.

"Hmm." She reached out a finger, following the path of moisture along his cock. "How fast is your recovery time?"

"Not as fast as it was when I was a teenager." He lay beside her, propping his head on a hand. "But I could make an exception for you."

"You seem to be making a lot of exceptions for me." Like being willing to settle in one place.

"Well, you're an exceptional woman, Jamie Walker." He kissed her, slow and sweet, his tongue dipping into her mouth. She turned in to him, eager for more. He curved his free hand around her breast, his thumb making a slow sweep across her beaded nipple. The soft cotton of her gown was almost abrasive on the sensitive flesh, and she shuddered. Grabbing the hem of her nightshirt, she tugged it off and tossed it aside. She needed to feel him against her.

He tried to roll her onto her back, but she resisted. "No. I want to touch you this time."

"By all means." He took her hand and laid it over his heart, the erratic beat telling her how much this affected him. "You won't mind if I do the same, will you?"

They explored each other. He kissed his way along her collarbone, across her shoulder. She slid a fingertip down the curve of his spine, cupped her palm over his ass. Touched him everywhere she could reach. She hadn't had the chance last night, and she wanted to make up for lost time. His groans told her what he liked the most—her mouth on the flat discs of his nipples, her fingers wrapped around his dick.

He eased his fingers into the thatch of curls between her thighs, teasing her clit while she stroked his cock. It felt amazing, but it wasn't enough. "I want you inside me."

"I thought you'd never ask." He groaned, jackknifing upward to make a grab for the condom. His fingers shook while he rolled it on, but then he drew her toward him, pulling one of her knees over his hip. They lay facing each other, the head of his dick pressed to her entrance. He paused, his gaze focusing on her face. "I meant to tell you…"

"What?" Her eyes widened. He was stopping *now*? Her body quivered with desire, her nails biting into his backside as she tried to urge him forward.

"I made some money rodeoing. More than some, actually." His expression was almost sheepish. "Never got around to spending it, so we can use that to expand the horse operation. I don't want you to think I'm trying to use—"

"We can talk about plans for the ranch *later*, Cord!" She slapped his ass. Hard. "*Hurry up.*"

A laugh spilled out of him. "Yes, ma'am."

He slid home in one swift thrust, and a low cry burst from her throat. Perfect. So perfect. She rocked her hips into his, and he matched her stroke for stroke. His gaze locked with hers, and she could see every emotion playing across his face. No tough cowboy here, just a man with needs. They moved faster and faster, their bodies bucking, grinding together. Her breathing was ragged gasps, sweat making their skin slippery. He rotated his pelvis against her clit, and orgasm crashed over her in a wave. Her inner muscles milked his cock, dragging him into climax with her. He shuddered, his fingers bruising as he gripped her thigh. They continued to move, dragging the sweet completion out as long as possible.

Contentment wound through her, and she finally relaxed against him, utterly spent.

"I love you." The words were quiet, solemn, but there was a tremor in his voice, as if he wasn't quite sure how his feelings might be received.

She cupped his face between her palms. "I love you too, Cord Preston. I have for a while now, but I didn't want to admit it because I knew you were leaving."

For a second, she thought she saw a sheen of tears in his dark eyes. He cleared his throat twice before he spoke. "Honey, you will never get rid of me. Nothing and no one has ever made me want to stay before. Until you…" He shook his head, offering a crooked smile. "I love you, Jamie. I've never said that to any woman until you."

She pulled him down and put every ounce of feeling she had into her kiss—happiness, desire, need, endless love. Life had given her many sorrows, but it had also handed her joy. Two strong, wonderful men had loved her. Not many women were so lucky. She was just glad she'd been smart enough to love them back. Tightening her arms around Cord's neck, she held him close, never intending to let him go.

She whispered against his lips. "Stay with me."

"Forever," he promised.

A SINGER WHO DOESN'T SING

Jeanette Grey

"So, what are you?" he asks. He's standing in the light of the open French doors, the city bustling down beneath him, pale golden sun making the contours of his chest seem to glow. The burning ember of his cigarette is black and gray and flaking, and the curls of smoke twist around his head when he blows.

"Excuse me?"

Flicking ash, he looks over his bare shoulder at her. She's standing there in the middle of her living room, dressed only in a robe and unsure what, precisely, he thinks he's still doing here.

He smirks and gestures around the room. "I know the kind of people who live in this part of town. So which one are you? A writer who doesn't write? A painter who doesn't paint?"

She follows the movements of his hand and restrains herself from commenting on the fall of ash on her hardwood floor. He's trying to say something about her space, so she takes it in, trying to see the place the way that someone else would. The color of the walls and the dust on all her books. The antique typewriter on the mantle and the canvases that are just as naked as his skin is—the ones she's been staring at for years now and has never gotten around to putting away.

His implication hits something tender in her chest, and she bristles, crossing her arms over her breasts. "Neither." She gave up on both of those a long, long time ago.

"Ah." He bends to put the cigarette out on the iron grating of her balcony, then turns to edge back inside. "A realist, then. Rare but not unappealing."

The space falls away like nothing at all, and suddenly he's in front of her, breathing her air, all heat and skin and a trail of fingertips heading toward the sash of her robe. She stutters and twists her head to the side as he runs his nose along the column of her throat. She just brought him home for a night; she just picked him up because he looked pretty in the blue and red lights of the bar. And he had been pretty. So pretty, all muscle and warmth and the source of a soreness between her legs that says she had a very, very nice time indeed.

But prettiness and a skilled, wicked tongue are not the things of a morning after, and he smells like smoke as well as man. She closes her eyes as she tips her chin up and lets him nip and lick his way to her ear while holding her mouth away.

"I hope you're not expecting me to kiss you after that." She waves her hand ineffectively toward the place on the balcony where what's left of his cigarette is still smoldering.

"No. But I expect you to let me *kiss* you." With that, he sinks to his knees.

"What—"

"Here." He pushes the sides of her robe up with ink-stained hands and parts her with his thumbs. The rasp of breath over bare, slickening flesh is warm and unexpected. She's never had it quite like this, not with her standing in the middle of a room, not with the man who should have slunk out in the middle of the night asking her what she is and threatening to make her forget regardless.

He lets her back away until her spine is to the wall, and then he's unyielding, shoulders fitting to the V of her thighs, tongue hot and wet against her clit and fingers pushing inside. Fucking her with his hand, he licks and licks and licks, and she puts her hands in his hair. She doesn't know what this is, doesn't know why he's going down on her, making her rise like the ball of the sun over her balcony, but she's no dummy. She pulls his face in closer and rides it. When he slings her leg over his shoulder, she lets him hold her up until she floats away.

She's still coming back down, still pulsing when he puts her on the floor, gets his fly down and protection on and gets inside. It's like her hips and shoulders are parts of the wood, like he's fucking her through the floor, and she just wraps her legs around him. He doesn't try to kiss her mouth, but his lips are on her nipple, his hands playing her ribs like piano keys, and how did he learn to make such music?

She comes around him, uncertain if she ever even really finished with the last one, and he asks her if it's good, if she could drown in this, and she could, she is, she *is*. He clasps her jaw in his hand and sinks his teeth into her neck, bucks once, then twice, then stills.

After, she lies with her head on his chest, staring out at the sky through the doors he left open when he didn't leave. Running the backs of her knuckles over his abdomen, she asks, "And what are you?"

He twirls an unlit cigarette between his fingertips. "I'm a singer who doesn't sing."

* * *

On Monday, she walks into her office to find a bouquet of red pencils, sitting on her desk.

"So?"

She hesitates, trailing a hand over the back of his couch. "It's...not quite what I expected."

Nothing about him is—not his invitation or his gifts or the way he looked at her over a plate of spaghetti before asking her back to his place.

It's a studio apartment in the bowels of the Village, and the tiny living space is dominated by an upright piano that takes up most of the main interior wall. Turning her back on him, she walks toward it and touches the cool ivory of the keys. A single, hollow note rings out, and it feels like the first one the place has heard in a while.

She looks at him and asks, "Do you play?"

"I already told you." His gait is loose and easy as he comes to stand beside her, pressing a kiss to the bare skin of her neck before pulling her down to sit with him on the bench. "Not anymore."

"Why not?"

Shrugging, he fiddles with the strap of her dress. He slides it down and runs rough fingertips over her collarbone. "It didn't feel like it was mine."

"Were you any good?"

"Good enough to almost make a living at it. And that was enough to kill it."

She knows the story as if it were her own. She thinks of deadlines and newsprint stains and the whir of the press. There were so many words she didn't care about and words she didn't mean, and none of them were hers by the time they'd been wrung out of her. She'd had no words left of her own.

"I'd love to hear you play sometime."

"I'd love to see what you can make."

She laughs as he drifts his hand lower, brushing it around the outer curve of her breast. He makes it easy, somehow, this intimacy with a not-quite-stranger. It makes her bold. She pushes his hand away, but it's only to straddle him, one knee to either side of his hips.

"To see what I can make beside love?" She murmurs it, sass and sex, with her lips just close enough to ghost across the corner of his mouth.

He nods and leans back, one hand on her thigh and the other at the small of her back. "*Besides* love."

But that's the only thing they make that night except for noise, except for the thump of the legs of the bench against the floor, except for the crash of his shoulders on ivory keys as she sinks down on him. He's hard and big and just as good as she remembers, and it's even better when he slips a hand between them, a plaintive middle C sounding out with every twitch of his forearm to stroke her where they're joined.

"And you said you didn't play anymore," she breathes, riding him hard. She slams her hands down on the keys for anything to hold on to.

He shakes his head and drives his hips up into hers. "I said I didn't play unless it felt like mine."

With his free hand curled possessively around her neck, she can't question him. She feels like his, feels like they could play this—could play each other—forever.

When she's almost at her peak, he reaches up and pulls the red pencil from her hair, undoing the twist, and the locks fall down around them like a curtain from the world. He kisses her mouth and he doesn't taste like smoke. "Sing for me."

She shatters like notes, shivering crystal to its bones. She crashes like hands clattering over piano keys. And when he pulls her down on him, groaning her name into her ear, it's music, indeed.

One year after she picked him up at a bar, he stands in front of their balcony, framed against the city's twinkling lights as the sun sets over the horizon. He hasn't lit up a cigarette in months, but sometimes she still thinks she smells them on him. She almost misses the curl of the smoke around his head and on his tongue.

One year, and still, a part of her is expecting him to leave, to disappear like so many ambitions and dreams that no longer feel like hers. He doesn't, though.

They're surrounded by boxes, and an upright piano now dominates the wall beside her dusty typewriter. The empty canvases are propped against the velvet-covered bench. They look good together, she thinks. Like they belong.

He walks over to her and wraps his arms around her waist, pulling her close. A soft peck behind her ear and a tug of teeth at the lobe. "Come to bed with me?"

"A little early for that, don't you think?"

"Not at all."

A giggle that doesn't sound like her but sounds exactly like them spills from her lips as he lifts her bridal style. Safe in his embrace, she holds on with one arm slung around his shoulder, her other hand tangled in his hair as she kisses his temple and buries her nose in soft locks.

He sets her down on their bed and comes to hover over her on hands and knees. He kisses her mouth, licking into it and chasing her tongue. Then he slides down. She arches her back and lets him pull at fabric with lips and teeth and fingertips.

Naked, she feels as real as she ever has beneath the solidity of his hands, and she spreads her legs.

"Kiss me?" she asks. She slides her fingertip down to swirl in a circle around her clit. "Here?"

He tugs his shirt off and shifts to lie on his stomach between her thighs. He's done this so many times, has ended up wet all over his mouth and down his chin, has dragged messy fingers over his own chest to rub her slick across his nipples and then to clasp around his cock before pressing in.

With a smirk, he presses kisses to the juncture of her leg and her hip, to the inside of her knee and the back of her wrist. He licks all around her fingers when she disappears them into her body, and then finally, finally, he purses his lips around her clit. She pulls her hand away, slides shining knuckles to rest on her belly. His hand comes up to splay beside hers, flat and broad and pushing her down when she wants to buck up into that soft, lapping heat.

And he knows how to do this so well now, knows how to twist and curl his fingers just inside, how to tease and how to make her writhe. She rises and rises with every deep push of his tongue, and she's digging fingernails into his shoulder, everything tight and set to break and—

"What?" She chokes on the word, clenching on nothing as her stomach plummets, so close it hurts; she's aching and swollen and *wants*.

"Shh. I know what you need." He kneels at the foot of the bed and pulls his belt free, opens his pants and shoves everything down, gets naked and then comes to lie over her. Sliding the tip of his cock around her opening, he gets himself nice and wet, and he's right there. Right there.

She can't stop the little whining noise, the hiss of satisfaction when he pushes inside, thick and perfect and bare. She curls her ankle around his calf and hitches the other leg. He puts his hand to the curve of her ass and slides it to the back of her thigh, pressing it higher, bending her and opening her, making her wide so he can drive in hard. He palms her flesh so easily, feels big and solid as he thrusts and grinds, and she's so full.

"Perfect," he murmurs, lips touching hers with each syllable.

With each glide of flesh, each rock of hips against hips, he gets her back to the top of that precipice, pressure just where she needs it as he stays flush, buried deep. He surges, the rhythm one she knows so well and yet still feels new. Brightness coils, then tingles of feeling and the promise of the rush of pleasure, the overtaking wave. When it finally hits her, it's tidal, pulling her under. She heaves and curls herself up, fixes her teeth to his shoulder and bites down hard.

He doesn't make her stop, just helps her through it, and when she's lax and easy again, opening her jaw for breath, he lets her leg go and wraps his fingers around her throat. It's light, no threat there as he pushes her back onto the mattress. He keeps his eyes open as his thrusts go long again, the steady pace of the way her fucks her slowly giving way until it's erratic and breathless, and she writes the words *I love you* on his skin as he closes his eyes.

He drops both palms to the mattress just before he tenses, before his voice breaks and he pulses, making everything wetter and warmer. He drags himself out and falls to his side, one arm curled loosely over her waist. With his face pressed to her shoulder, he breathes and breathes and breathes, and she thinks maybe she can keep this. Maybe this is what she needed, and maybe it's just for her.

Coming back to himself, he lifts his face and presses a kiss to the point of her jaw. It's so simple, comfortable in a way she never expected intimacy to be. She never expected to be this happy.

He rolls onto his back, tugging her to move with him. She ends up lying on her side, head tucked up under his chin, staring at her own hand as she traces invisible lines against his side, feeling wrapped up and safe.

He breaks the silence, asking quietly, voice rough, "That first night. Why did you pick me?"

The whole scene at the bar has morphed over the course of this year. What she once thought of as just a whim she now sees in softer hues. He was pretty; he still is. But there was more to it than that. She'd liked the way he moved, as if he were part of the beat.

She gets the words out before she can stop them. "Because I saw music under your skin."

Humming, he lets out a little chuckle and closes his hand around her side.

The silence only lasts a minute this time before she clears her throat. "That first morning. Why did you stay?"

He drags his knuckles over her cheek. "Because I heard paintings under yours."

She smiles and nestles in deeper.

At some point, she drifts off to the feeling of his fingers playing music on her ribs. She wakes to a dark room, to full night beyond the open curtains of her window.

She wakes to the sound of a song.

She finds the robe she wore their first morning together and pulls it on, tying the sash at her waist and hugging herself against the chill as she tiptoes out into the living room.

He's there, hair in his eyes, long fingers arched as they make chords and trills of notes that fill the room. As he opens his mouth, the softest baritone sweeps over her. And she knows him. She knows him as well as she's ever known a lover, knows the taste of his mouth and the weight of his body and the cadence of his thoughts.

On another level, though, she's never known him before this moment.

He's beautiful, gorgeous in lines and shades and shadow-drenched planes, and she doesn't want to interrupt him. Doesn't want to change anything about this moment except to make it last.

She wants to *make* something.

From the jar of pencils on the console, she withdraws one with a dull red barrel, scratched and bitten and worn from a year of use. She finds a notebook under one of the piles. With quiet steps, she makes her way over to their couch and sits, tucking bare feet under the corner of a cushion to keep them warm, and opens the notebook to a page that's as naked as she was, moments before. A page that's as naked as she feels.

She wets the tip of the pencil with her tongue. And then she begins to draw.

SHOW ME

D. R. Slaten

I could feel his eyes on me. I could feel how they moved over me. I knew what he saw. Just as I knew what he wanted.

The heat of his gaze shot through me.

He remained quiet. Watching. Waiting. Still. As if the slightest noise, the most minute of movements would spook me.

It probably would. I was nervous. Scared. I felt laid open. Completely bared. Not just naked but *naked*.

I had never done anything like this before. Wasn't real sure I would do anything like this again. If you asked me where I got the nerve, I wouldn't be able to tell you. I wasn't that girl. I just wasn't.

It might have been the day. It was so hot outside that the asphalt was sending up waves of heat. It was a lazy day, not by choice but by necessity. It was the kind of heat for which the siesta was invented.

It might have been the time. Not quite midday. Not quite early evening. It was the in-between time. The point in the day that went from being high energy to just winding down.

It might have been the sun. It lay heavy in the sky. It was just moving down, fighting the slow slide into the horizon.

Nothing made sense. Nothing tipped me off as to why I was willing to do what I was doing, when I had balked before.

I was sweating. As much from the heat outside as from the heat within me. I watched as a drop of sweat rolled down from my collarbone through the valley of my breasts and then wound its way to my belly button where it got captured. Lost in the deep groove.

I walked slowly over to my bed. The bed reflected an aspect of my personality that had never surfaced. Not in real life. The deep-red color, the luxuriousness of the fabric, the softness of the feather bed. It screamed of a sensuality that I wasn't sure I possessed.

Except today. Apparently I possessed that sensuality today. Today I was willing to step out of my comfort zone. Today, I was willing to own that I was a sensual, sometimes wanton creature.

Nothing about the day was overly special. Nothing about it screamed now. Let it be now.

I lay down on my bed, smoothing my hands over the rich, soft velvet duvet and feeling how it covered an equally soft down comforter as my hands sank into it. So soft. I stopped to enjoy the tactile feel of it in my hands.

I slid on my belly the final few inches that would allow me to stretch out completely. Caressing my entire body and rubbing my nipples over the fabric. The friction from the slide creating more heat. Without and within.

My body screamed for more. But I was in no hurry. I savored. Sipped of pleasure. Tasting it slowly.

I felt my nipples catch as they pebbled from the contact. At the shot of arousal, I burrowed my head into the pillow and took a breath to slow down my drumming heart. It didn't help. My heart continued to be beat hard and loud.

I slowly rolled over. Cupping my breasts as I spread my legs. Exposed. Bare.

"Show me," he whispered. So softly that I had to strain to hear the words he spoke. "Let me see, baby. Show me more."

I kept my eyes downcast. I couldn't look at him. My nerve wouldn't have withstood his direct gaze.

I hadn't realized how much I would like his eyes on my body, watching me. But even as I knew that I liked that he stared at me, I still couldn't look at him.

I took one of my hands from my breasts, leaving the other to tug and pull on my nipple. I slid my finger through the wetness coating the inside of my thighs. Brushing past my clit, jerking when I did. My juices had been leaking since I walked out from the bathroom. I knew I would leave a spot. I didn't care. It was a small price to pay for the largeness of what I felt.

My pussy had flowered. My inner lips spread outward in enticement, in invitation. I let my finger glide between my inner lips to reach the heart of me. The entrance that wept in welcome. I pushed one finger, then two into me. I let the heel of my hand move against my clit, pressing that button until I could feel the contractions within me.

I mimicked the sexual act with my fingers, pumping them in and out. Each time I pulled out, I brought more wetness with me.

I could hear his breath increase, watching me. I knew that his eyes were focused between my legs. I heard the rasp of his zipper as he unzipped his pants.

If I had looked up, I would have been able to see him take out his cock. Instead I remained with my eyes averted. I could only imagine his beautiful cock pulled out of his pants. His hands on himself as mine were on me.

That he liked what I was doing enough to have to take himself in hand added to my arousal. His pleasure gave me pleasure. Knowing that it was my pleasure that began his tripped my triggers. Almost too much.

I pulled harder on my nipples. I could feel each pull deep in my pussy. So deep, my fingers couldn't reach that far.

"Finish it, baby." His whispered voice still held the element of command.

How he could tell that I needed more was mystifying. But he did. And I did.

I pulled my fingers from my pussy and dragged them back up toward my clit. Slowly at first, I circled it. I was dripping wet. Which made stimulating my clit both easier and harder all at the same time.

As the pressure built, as the pleasure grew, my fingers moved faster. Not harder. Not softer. Just faster. I pulled and rolled my nipple in time with my fingers on my clit. Both my hands working to bring me over.

I could feel the buildup, the tension within me stretching tight. My womb contracting so violently that my lower belly rippled.

I was poised on the edge of the precipice. Riding the crest of the coming waves of orgasm. I held it back as long as I could. I wanted to hold on to the feeling. I didn't want to let it go.

It was his soft groan that tipped my want into need. Then I let it go. And wave upon wave of contractions took me from almost there, to there. I was there. I moaned, the exhalation of pent-up need released all at once.

It was at the moment of my climax that my eyes flew up to stare at him. I had to look at him, my eyes widening in shocked pleasure, as if I had never experienced orgasm before. He stared at my mouth as it opened to moan.

My body jerked as I continued to work my clit. I rubbed my palm over my beaded nipple, milking every last drop from my body.

"Beautiful Dani," he said and moved toward me.

His face went to my pussy. He drank from me then. Lapping up my wetness like the offering it was. I had come for him.

He moved up my body once he had his fill. Kissing my belly, dipping his tongue into the crevice that the drop of salty sweat had disappeared into. He licked and sucked my nipples until they both glistened from his mouth, tightened in a way they never did just for me.

He kissed my throat, my neck and finally...finally my mouth. I tasted myself on his tongue. I tasted him as well. The taste of the two of us together was delicious.

"Thank you," he said.

I knew his thank-you was my reward for being brave enough to let him watch me masturbate. He had been asking for a while. He wanted to see how I pleasured myself. He wanted to know how I brought myself off. He was interested in what I did and how I did it. And he was interested in how I touched myself so that he could learn what I liked, as much as he was just interested in watching me do it. Maybe more.

If he had loved watching me half as much as I love watching him, then it was all good. It almost seems like I can feel it when he strokes himself in front of me. He is not shy about touching himself. Not at all.

"I didn't think it would turn me on as much as it did. To do that for you. To let you see me," I told him.

"Yeah?" he asked. His eyes were still hot. Hotter even than it was outside. "Why today?"

"Not sure. I just felt it. The heat is getting to me. I didn't want to put clothes on after the shower. I saw you in the hallway. Then my brain just jumped right in and said, now, show him now," I confessed.

He was still hard and hot against me. He had held back when I came. I could feel him rubbing against me.

"I need to fuck you, Dani. But if I get inside you right now, with the vision of you fucking yourself, I'll come as soon as I enter you," he told me.

His cock was leaving a trail of precum on my leg, helping it glide against my skin. Although with my sweat already there, his precum wasn't really necessary.

I trailed my fingers down the side of his body. My thumb caressed his hip bone and began to move toward his cock. I wanted to touch him. To stroke him.

"Hands above your head, Dani. Grab the headboard," he told me. "If you touch me now, it'll all be over."

I removed my hands from him and reached above my head to comply. The position arched my back and pressed my breasts against his chest. The small amount of chest hair he had was teasing me. I moved slowly back and forth to increase the sensation.

I had just come, but I was still aroused. Incredibly aroused. It might have been my thoughts of him watching me as I brought myself off, or it might have been the thought of him about to fuck me. It probably was a combination of both.

I could feel the wetness between my legs pooling underneath my ass. I was ready for him now. Had been ready for a while.

Still, I waited. Waited for him to be ready as well.

He made my wait worthwhile.

He grasped his cock by the root and fitted himself against my entrance. There was more than enough wetness between his leaking cock and the copious amount of juices flowing from my pussy.

He snapped his hips and entered me in one hard thrust.

Full, I was so full. He stilled as he fully embedded himself in me. Everything stopped. My perception of time had come to a standstill. All that existed was me at the place where he joined me. That point was the center, the entirety of my universe.

I loved how he felt in me. I loved how I felt when he covered me. I loved him.

He looked deep into my eyes. I felt his stillness as I stayed motionless, my hands still grasping the headboard. I savored the moment, our connection.

Then he began to move. Not tentative, shallow thrusts designed for exploration but full, hard thrusts that pounded his cock into my body. He didn't fuck me fast. He moved with purpose. Steadily, drawing almost completely out of my pussy and then pushing right back in.

His body moved; his eyes did not. He kept his eyes on me the entire time. I looked right back at him. In this, I could look my fill. My eyes were caught by his.

"I can't last much longer, Dani. I wanted to bring you off again, but I'm too keyed up from watching you play with your pussy, babe," he gritted out.

Now he was sweating too. Drops of his sweat fell onto my face. I licked them up. Then I licked his lips. I pushed my tongue into his mouth. I wanted him to lose control. I wanted to be the one that made him lose it.

I knew that I had succeeded when he began to move faster. He was pistoning in and out of me. The heat from the friction seeping through my pussy into my body.

He threw back his head and groaned. His cock jerked inside me. I could feel him swell in preparation to fill me with his seed. Homage. I welcomed it. I wanted him to fill me with the evidence of his pleasure. His pleasure was my pleasure.

He gave tiny little jerks as he continued to come inside me. His mouth claiming mine as he finished.

His soft sigh signaling the end even as the aftershocks continued to make him twitch.

He finally pulled out of me. He got up and grabbed a wash-cloth. Then he cleaned us both. He threw the rag back toward the bathroom and crawled back into bed next to me.

"That was wow. Just fucking wow," he sighed.

I snuggled into him. "I could so totally go for a nap right about now."

"Not gonna happen, babe," he told me, even as he drew me into his side.

I played with his six-pack, following his happy trail back up over his chest. "Why not?"

"Got dinner at my mom's tonight, remember?" was his response.

"Oh shit." I tried to jump up. His arms tightened around me. "I can't go to your mom's tonight."

"Why not?" he asked again.

"'Cause my face will be on fire remembering what I did for you this afternoon. I can't go to your mom's right after I mastur-bated for you," I tell him.

He grins at me. "Babe, you already masturbated. Any time we go to my mom's now will be after you masturbated for me."

"It's not the same," I tell him. "Maybe we can have her over. Like next week or month or year. Or far enough out that I won't turn beet fucking red from my hussy-like behavior."

I am snapping at him. I think having his mom over is perfect. We've only been living together for a few months, only having known each other a couple of months before that. It was quick.

But I was sure. He had told me he was as well, when he asked me to move in.

I had only met his mom once. Now that I was thinking about it, he had done dirty, dirty things to me before that time as well. Maybe his mom was a catalyst for my naughty side to emerge. Shit, what if she knew the things he did to me? How could I look the woman who gave birth to him in the eye ever again?

"I like you dirty, Dani. You're dirty because of me. No reason for you to get all bent about it," he says matter of factly.

"Don't mind being dirty with you either Ian. Just don't want the interval between being dirty and seeing your mom to be like zero-point-two seconds." He was irritating me with his nonchalance.

He grins bigger. "You're cute, babe."

Argh. I think blood vessels in my head broke wide open when he said that.

"We're not fucking ever again on the days we're supposed to meet up with your mom," I declare, ignoring how much he was irritating me by his thinking my mini-meltdown was funny.

It was so not funny.

"Babe, my mom is already clued in that I like to fuck. She knows that I like you. She's smart. Putting all that together, whether we fuck the day of, she's still gonna know we fuck," he tells me.

"Oh my god," I almost scream.

He kisses me then. The spool-up I had going on cooled.

"Babe, go shower again. Then we go. I need to stop off and grab some beer." He smacks my ass to punctuate his point.

I waver. I'm screwed either way. I might as well give in gracefully. With that decided, I get up and go toward the shower.

It's too hot to stay upset for any length of time anyway.

I turn back to him. "You love me?"

"Yeah, babe." He doesn't hesitate to confirm this.

"Come shower with me," I say to him. Then I pause until he looks at me again. "I love you too."

His face softens and his smile stays. "Be right there."

"But no fucking in the shower," I tell him. "I don't need that to think about as well when we go over to your mom's."

He busts out laughing.

"We'll see, Dani."

A PERFECT PLACE

Catherine Paulssen

I step outside the palace at the outskirts of Vienna when my phone rings. It's Alicia, my boss, and I can tell immediately that she's not as calm as her tone pretends. "Hon, I'm on the phone with Alexander and I just told him we've found the perfect place for the movie."

"What do *you* think, Julie?" Alexander's voice calls through the speaker.

I take a deep breath and think about a way to start, but before I can even utter a word, he cuts me off. "I see. Well, all right."

I bite back a little smile, even though Alicia can't see me anyway. Alexander's one of the busiest directors I've ever worked for. I guess picking up the gist of a situation within moments comes with his schedule. He has no time for beating around the bush.

"Alexander"—Alicia chimes in—"don't you want to see the photos Julie has taken first, or hear what she has to—"

"No." He exhales. "Listen, one of the producers just met this guy whose family apparently owns half of Hungary. He says they have an old castle on a mountain that might be just the thing we're looking for. Have a look at it, will you? I'll tell Kelsey to give you his number."

While I listen to Alexander's assistant and scribble down the Hungarian guy's contact information, I steel myself for a peeved call from Alicia. And as reliable as clockwork, the moment I've hung up, my phone rings again.

"One word!" she says. "If you had given him one word, this endless marathon all across Europe would finally be over."

"It wasn't the right location."

"And why not? 'The neoclassical *Palais Schönburg*, built in 1790, is one of the finest examples of Vienna's architectural treasures. Today, it's most famous for its wall frescos and enchanted gardens...' blah blah blah," she reads from a memo. "That's *just* what they were looking for!"

"Licia, how long has Alexander been working with us now?"

"About what—eight years?"

"Ten," I say, trying hard not to sound too smug. "Ten years. You want it to stay that way, right? Trust me, he wouldn't have been satisfied." I glance back at the salmon-colored palace. "The ground and exteriors are great, but inside it was too—neat. It lacked dilapidation; I can't really explain. But I know for certain it's not the right place for the movie."

She sighs. "Fine. Call me when you're in Hungary, okay?"

I promise and hail a cab.

The next day, I take the train from Budapest south to a small village in the Baranya County. A meeting has been arranged by the estate's secretary, and some Mr Illésházy will meet me at the market square in front of the only church. I assume he's the administrator and for some reason, picture a good-humoured, middle-aged man with a gray moustache.

If the castle proves to be the location Alexander's looking for, maybe I can persuade Alicia to let me stay in Hungary for another day. Everyone has been exquisitely nice to me, and the countryside is the embodiment of rural idyll. The train passes fields of wheat ready for harvesting and big trees whose branches are abundant with apples and pears. Gentle slopes, covered with long culms that sway in a gentle breeze, become densely forested hills, and sometimes, I can catch a glimpse of the Danube in the east, sparkling in the July sun. At every village we stop at, I want to get off and wander around. You never know what hidden spots you may discover, or in my case, store away in an inner database as a possible location to come back to later.

My life is lived in trains, planes and taxicabs. I'm always on the lookout for the perfect background to a story, the scenery that grounds a character or sets him free. The place where love can blossom. Where dreams are being born, realized or taken to an early grave. Where families unite or the seed for divorce is being sown. My own place is the road, and that fits *my* character and my life as a location scout to one of Europe's biggest production companies.

I arrive at the small village in the afternoon, and it's easy to find the whitewashed church that presides over a cobblestoned market square. There's only one car parked in front of it, and apart from me, some tourists, two women chatting and children playing hopscotch. No one who appears to be waiting for me.

"Ms. Scott?"

I turn and face a man in his midthirties, tall and black-haired. "Mr Illésházy?" He nods and gives me a little smile. He has the most beautiful eyes I've ever seen in a man. Dark brown, with little twinkles in them, framed by strong brows and prominent cheekbones.

I need to stop gawping. "So you're the administrator?"

"No, I...I believe my uncle's a friend of one of the producers for your movie?"

"Oh!" Great. Ten seconds, and I've already embarrassed myself and offended one of the estate's owners. "Oh, I'm very sorry. It's nice to meet you."

He shakes my hand, a quirk of humor in his eyebrow. "Welcome to Hungary." His English has a light accent that gives an alluring edge to the way he speaks. "Please," he says and opens the car door.

He doesn't say a word while we drive out of the village. The fields around the village get replaced by woodland, and soon, we are on top of a rise that's the first in a chain of wooded hills. "So all of this belongs to your family?"

He nods. "We have a lot of land, but not a lot of cash." I look at him, but there's no trace of bitterness in his features. "So there's not much maintenance."

I check out his face, the strong arms revealed by the rolled-up sleeves of his shirt, as tanned as the rest of his skin. "Have you been living here all your life?"

He nods. I wait for him to add something, or pose a question in return, but he simply stares at the road ahead.

"It must have been wonderful to grow up here," I say, after the period of silence has become long enough to cross the line to awkwardness.

"Don't feel obliged," he says.

"I'm sorry?"

"You don't have to make conversation, Ms. Scott." He smiles politely, but decisively. My cheeks grow hot. I think he catches my expression, because after a short pause, he points toward a mountain range in the distance. "Over there you can see the Mecsek Mountains. Very important in the history of this country."

I square my shoulders and stare at the dark hills. "Call me Julie, please. If that wouldn't be too shallow."

"I'm Benedek."

I keep my eyes fixed on the mountains, but I can hear the grin in his voice. I only hope the place is more promising than meeting its owner.

The forest eventually gives way to an alley lined with plane trees. At its end, behind a wrought-iron gate with gilt accenting, lies a yellowish, three-story mansion. In its center, a steeple cupola rises above black roof tiles. The sun is swallowed by windows so dull with dirt and dust they are almost blind. Poppies grow along the weather-worn walls, and the two statues at the end of the driveway are covered with moss. Gravel scrunches underneath the car's wheels as Benedek drives toward a majestic stairway that leads to the entrance door.

He trails behind me while I take photos of the building's front and the entry area. I can't get the strange car ride out of my head, and it takes all my professionalism to focus on getting all the necessary pictures. The distance he keeps is appropriate enough, but I can feel his eyes on me. The inkling of being watched tickles in my neck and even the tips of my fingers.

"On the left are old stables where equipment can be stored. They have electricity and water connections," he says. "Speaking of which, the fountains are still working," he adds and points to a dried-up basin with a lion in its center.

I gladly jump at the distraction. Finally, I'm on safe ground, and Benedek answers all my questions regarding the property with precision and good will.

I relax a little when we step inside. The air of the entrance hall is cool, slightly damp and a great relief to my hot skin. I follow Benedek up a grand staircase to the first floor where he leads me to the former reception room. The furniture is arranged as if a big party was expected, but everything—chairs, an oval table, a piano—is covered by white sheets.

I take pictures of the fading arras tapestry, a grand chandelier, its sparkle long gone, and my pulse beats a little quicker. Usually, when I'm in decaying places, I do a quick fix-up in my head. It's a program that's set into motion by default. I think what great lofts the nineteenth-century coal-mine buildings would make. How the check some Middle Eastern oil heir would write for a Scottish castle would be worth three times the sum necessary to restore it. That a derelict windmill could easily be turned into a charming party venue.

With this place, it's different. No pictures start running in my head. I'd leave everything exactly like it is.

"What is it?" Benedek interrupts my musings.

"Pardon?"

"You..." He gestures at his forehead. "You frowned."

I blush. "It's just..." I take a deep breath. "I thought of the set decorators and the camera crews and all the equipment rolling through the corridors."

He regards me with a little smile. I stride to the other side of the room and open a window. Paint flakes off the frame. The air that streams in from outside smells of flowers and dry grass.

He steps to one of the windows next to mine. "Tell me about the movie."

I take a few pictures of the yard stretching out below. "There's this girl who inherits an old castle in the countryside.

When she gets to the place, she discovers a dark secret that has to do with the romance of a family member, decades ago. She eventually solves it, together with a guy from the village. There's a lot of mystery and…" I turn my head toward him and shrug. "Of course, love."

From his place a few feet away, he looks at me with a quizzical expression on his face. "Why do you say it like that?"

"Say what like that?"

"*Love*," he says, with a simplicity as if it was the most natural thing in the world. I throw him a baffled look. Is this the guy who didn't want to talk only two hours ago? "Don't you know love?" he asks.

"Of course I know love," I retort, but the words don't come out of my mouth as sharply as I'd like them to.

Benedek's face doesn't change. He stays quiet for a while. "Don't you believe in it then?"

I don't know what to reply. This is the strangest conversation I've ever had with a potential client, or with a man, come to think of it. And yet I'm intrigued. Do I believe in love? I open my mouth, but still, no words come out.

"What about passion?" he asks. All I can do is nod. He takes a couple of steps toward me, closing the gap between us.

"I believe in passion," I croak. He takes the camera out of my hand and places it on a nearby chair. Butterflies start twirling in my stomach. He slides his fingers under my chin and lifts my face. His jeans rub against my leg. Apprehension's gripping my throat, and the blood rushing against my temples is the only sound I hear. I stare at his slightly parted lips. "What about you?" I whisper.

"Passion?" he asks. His face is so close now that our breath mingles. I swallow. A playful smile tugs at the corner of his mouth. Instead of answering, he closes his eyes and next, his lips are on mine. He tastes of olives and herbs. His skin is smooth and fresh, as if he had only shaved shortly before our appointment. His arms tighten around me and pull me up against him as he deepens the kiss. I let myself fall into his embrace, and I don't open my eyes again for what might be minutes or hours. The sudden ring of my phone breaks the spell he's put me under. I blink into the sun that stands low over the hills now and make a move for my bag. Benedek takes my hand.

"That might be my boss," I object, but he entwines our fingers. He presses a fleeting kiss on my cheeks and moves his lips to my ears. The ringing eventually stops, and I snuggle up to him. "I need to make photos of the gardens before it gets dark," I sigh into his shirt. The phone call conjured up a very vivid image of Alicia pacing her desk, and of the harangue she'll give me.

"You can come back tomorrow," he whispers. "Or stay the night."

My heart's pounding against my chest. I wrap my arms a little tighter around him. "I guess I could do that," I murmur.

Benedek kisses my hair, then he gets down on his knees and runs his hands along my calves. He takes off my pumps. His fingers wander up my legs again until they reach the lacy end of my holdups. He circles my thigh with his fingertips, and begins to roll down first the left stocking, then the right one, languidly tracing the shape of my legs, lingering a little at the back of my knees. He reaches around me to unzip my skirt. With a soft swishing sound, it falls on the floor. I silently congratulate myself for deciding to wear a black thong today. Without a word, Benedek unbuttons my blouse. He holds my gaze and I wonder if he can smell my arousal. If he does, he gives no sign of noticing it.

He cups my face, kisses me, then removes the hair slide that pins up my hair. His eyes follow the movement of my hair as it falls down my shoulders. He makes me step out of the thong and opens my bra. My body's covered in goose bumps despite the sunbeams that fall through the open window. Lastly, he undoes the clasp of my necklace and with a muffled noise, it lands on the pile of my clothes.

I stand before him, naked, but instead of touching or kissing the body that's all his for the taking, Benedek steps back. He can't miss the little shiver that runs through my body and tenses my nipples. They are so hard already that I wonder why he doesn't just wrap his lips around them, suck, lick, kiss them. He has been good at reading my mind so far, even when I had less obvious thoughts. I throw a quick glance at his jeans, and notice with satisfaction the bulge over his crotch.

Before I can act on that reassuring discovery, he walks to a piece of furniture, pulls away the huge sheet that covers it and wraps it around me, once, twice, before fastening it with a tight knot on the side. He steps out of his canvas shoes, opens his shirt and reveals a smooth chest underneath. "Come," he says and takes my hand.

The sheet is too long and rushes over the floor behind me like a train. At a pace that's much too ambling for my taste right now, we make our way through long corridors, past oil paintings and stained mirrors. I feel like a princess. A wicked princess, mind you. I'm completely naked underneath my gown, and I want so much more than a chaste kiss from the prince.

The hardwood floor creaks underneath our steps: my stumpy toes, with small dots of raspberry-red nail varnish, looking even more chubby next to his slender, bony feet, their skin the same caramel color as the rest of his body.

I can't wait to see all of him.

Finally, Benedek stops at a dove-colored tapestry with

golden ornaments. He reaches for a small key, and only now do I detect a small handle in the flowery pattern. He brushes my hair behind my shoulders and gives me a long kiss. The key creaks in the lock and the door opens to a narrow, beaten staircase. He holds my hand as I stumble through the twilight. At its end shines a bright light and I can spot a joist ceiling. We reach the end of the stairs and I realize that we're in the steeple cupola on the mansion's rooftop. It's hot up here, and it smells of old wood warmed by the sun. The whole room gleams in the setting sun's light. Benedek opens a French door to the gallery leading around the cupola. He pulls the sheets from an armchair, a side table, a small cupboard, and with every piece of furniture he reveals, the room's former splendor comes to life again. Dust particles dance in the sunbeams, irritating my throat, but all my attention is caught by the huge bed that emerges now. It has a simple, refined, hazel-colored frame and a thick mattress covered in a green velveteen case.

Benedek sits down on the bed and motions me to him. He unwraps the sheet and pulls me closer to him. His breath tickles my skin. He kisses my belly, and his lips move over my stomach, up to my breasts. They trace every piece of skin they can reach and finally, seize my nipples. He encloses one and his arms hold me tightly as my knees get weak. One arm firmly around my waist, he moves his other hand between my legs. I arch my pelvis forward, pressing my pussy against his hand, and he obliges me. Long, deliberate strokes caress my pussy lips and circle my clit. He places more kisses on my stomach, starts licking at my belly button and rubs his nose over my skin. My moans are only sighs now, and they grow more and more frantic. Benedek stops his treat; he kisses a spot just above the hairline of my delta and lays me down on the bed. I pant and catch my breath while he undresses.

His smile shows only a hint of self-consciousness as he finally stands before the bed, bare-naked. I sit up and crawl to the edge of the bed. He moans when I cup his balls. I slide up to his body so that my breasts rub against his chest, and explore him with my lips: his nipples, his neck, his collarbone, the pits of his arms. His cock pokes my thigh. He buries his face in my hair and his moans become muffled breaths that are hot against my scalp.

I cover his body in kisses and taste the summer day on his skin, the warmth, the salt, the scent of Benedek.

When I continue to ignore his pleadings, he swoops me up in his arms and we lie down, entangled with each other. His lips find mine again, his fingers run over my body, along my waist. He cups one of my breasts in his palm and rolls me over. Little kisses are placed on my neck while his hand fondles my breast. He treats my body the way he has been treating me the whole day, with calm, focused attention. The need for me glimmers in his eyes, underneath the affection, but his caress is tender, so tender I wonder how he's able to hold back. And why.

"Please, Benedek..." I pant. "Let go." He looks up. "I need you to let go," I repeat and kiss him hard. My teeth graze his bottom lip, and I gently bite his lip.

He continues to stare at me, his breath heavy and hot on my cheeks. "Please..." I say again, and after another moment, the restraint vanishes from his eyes. He bends my arms above my head and pins me down. With a quick move, he licks over my lips. I raise my head, but Benedek retreats. He lowers his face again, presses a kiss on my lip and retreats once more. I whimper with frustration, and only now does he really kiss me. His tongue explores my mouth, lures me to follow it, and the grip of his hands around my wrists loosens.

I throw back my head as his lips wander down my body. His

tongue flickers over my nipple, his hand slips between my thighs. He finds my clit, he tweaks it, rolls it between his fingers, presses his thumb against it and makes me wait before he resumes the tease of his fingers. His eyes are dark now, his jawline tensed. Two fingers are pushed inside of me, and I scream as he crooks them and finds the spot that can send me over the edge.

He moves his fingers inside of me until I'm a bundle of whispers and moans in his arms. He pulls away, making me whimper once more, then he pushes himself inside of me, easily.

He stays still for a moment. I wonder if he wants me to beg, but when I open my eyes, the look on his face is tender and tamed. He strokes my temple with the back of his hand and starts rocking me slowly. A tremor runs through his body and resonates with mine. His body thrums with energy as he finds a rhythm in which we lose ourselves. The high builds in the pit of my stomach. I bury my fingers in Benedek's back, hoping with the last thought I can control that I won't scratch him too hard.

The air is heavy with gold and warmth. The last rays of sunshine bathe our writhing bodies in a flaming red shimmer, setting us ablaze. The sound of my name pierces the air and it takes me some moments to realize it was Benedek, calling out to me as he collapses in my arms.

I lie still, my face tucked against his chest, and watch the pink clouds turn colorless over the Mecsek Mountains. Crickets chirp in the gardens, and the air is getting crisp. I wrap myself around him. He draws lazy circles on my back with his thumb, and when they stop, I assume he's fallen asleep. My eyes are heavy too, despite the exhilaration still running through my veins.

"Julie?" he suddenly says, and props himself up on his arm.

I open my eyes and look into his face. I could get used to hearing my name said with that sexy Hungarian accent.

"Do you think you've found the place you were looking for?" His eyes search mine.

I think about his question for a few moments. There are so many answers I could give him. There are so many ways he could have meant it. Eventually, I tilt my head and lean in so I can reach his ear. "It's a perfect place," I whisper, and place a kiss on his cheek. His mouth curls into a little smile. The delirious feeling that radiates from his smile makes my heart pound. "This chamber... Can it stay our secret?"

He reaches up to touch my face, traces lightly across my cheek and brushes a strand of hair behind my ears. "No camera crews rolling through?" he asks.

I nod. He rolls over and fumbles around with his clothes, scattered on the floor next to the bed. When he turns back to me again, there's a mischievous twinkle in his eyes. He opens my hand and places a small item into my palm. My heart races even harder. It's the brazen key that opens the tapestry door. "Take good care of it," Benedek whispers. He closes my fingers around it, smirks and leans over to kiss me.

SOMETHING NEW

Giselle Renarde

"Any new ideas?" Elson asked.

He always pushed her to dream up something new, something they'd never tried before. Something they'd never even *discussed*.

"I don't know." Kim cradled the phone against her shoulder and fluffed her pillows. "Let me think for a sec."

It wasn't easy coming up with some kinky new move for each visit. In truth, Kim would have been happy with a straightforward fuck. She liked fucking. It was easy—he got on top, she spread her legs. Towering over her, he rutted like an animal until he filled her with come. Why couldn't they do that all the time?

"Hey, why don't we save *something new* for the wedding night?" Kim nestled into bed. The sheets were cold, and she loved how fresh they felt against her warm skin. "That'd be a nice treat, to go all out when we're finally married."

That should buy her some time.

"I can't wait that long." There was a pained sort of urgency in Elson's voice. "You living with your parents is driving me nuts. I think about you constantly. I sit at work and think about your pussy. And your mouth! Holy fuck, Kim, I pretend you're kneeling under my desk, begging me to unzip. Can you imagine sucking my cock in my office?"

"Enough, Elson. I'm on the house line." Her voice came across harsh, but she worried one of her parents would pick up the phone and overhear these dirty words.

"See? Case in point." He sounded more dismayed than disgruntled. "When you had your own place you never worried about what I said over the phone. Hell, you got dirtier than me half the time."

Kim laughed. "No I didn't."

"Well, you got pretty damn dirty. Remember that time you called me at two in the morning and begged me to spank your ass raw?"

"Elson!" She tried to shush him but couldn't make the *shh* sound because she was giggling too much. "Oh my god, I was so drunk that night."

"I'd like to spank your ass right now." Elson made a hissing sound over the phone, like the very thought was torture. "Your butt would burn. You'd wake the whole neighborhood screaming for me to stop."

Kim's pussy pulsed, and she reached under the covers to cup her mound. "But you know why I moved back. You know how much money I'm saving in rent. It's not for *me*, it's for *us*. The more I save now, the more we can put down on a house."

He was quiet for a while, feeling suitably chastised, Kim hoped.

"I know," Elson finally said. "You're right, it's just hard. It puts such a cramp on our love life. You should spend your nights at my place. Do you honestly think your parents believe you're a virgin at thirty-two?"

"Yes," she shot back. "It's stupid, but you're always your father's daughter, you know?"

Of course Elson didn't know. How could he possibly understand?

"You're still coming over tomorrow, right?"

"Yes." Her clit throbbed at the thought of his big body on top of hers, that firm cock thrusting deep in her cunt. "Can't wait."

"So, what should we do that's new?" When she didn't answer, he said, "Come up with something or I'm driving out there right now and crawling in your bedroom window."

"Yeah right." Pussy juice soaked her lips, beckoning her fingers. "Okay, I know what you can do."

"Spank your ass raw?"

She could hear his smirk, and it pleased her. "That too, but you can also eat my pussy until I can't breathe—and then eat it some more."

His voice was gritty when he growled, "God, I want you."

"Tomorrow?"

"Now..."

"Tomorrow." She made kissing noises into the phone and then laughed. "Love you."

When they'd said their good nights and hung up, Kim kissed the phone and flicked off the bedside lamp. Her hand still cupped her mound, two fingertips playing in the juice of her arousal. She wanted to come. She wanted it now, but she just couldn't masturbate under her parents' roof. Her pussy throbbed, a wet heat, like it had its own heartbeat. She squeezed her mound hard, so hard her clit popped out between her slick lips. It was begging...begging...

Kim pulled her hand out from under the covers. Her fingers were slick with juice. *Save it for tomorrow. You can do this. You can wait.*

The whole thing happened in a whirlwind, right from the moment she burst into Elson's bachelor apartment. Instantly, she found herself in his arms. They kissed with such blazing intensity she thought their mouths might weld themselves together. Her pussy hadn't stopped begging all night, and her clit was now so blatantly engorged she moaned when the seam of her jeans pressed against her panties.

"If you don't eat me soon I'm gonna fucking scream."

"You're gonna scream either way." Elson tore off her top, and then stripped out of his robe. He was naked underneath, his cock so hard it stared right up at her. "You're gonna scream so loud we'll have the neighbors banging on the walls."

Kim fumbled with the button on her jeans. Her hands were trembling, but she couldn't get her pants off fast enough. Elson laughed at her striped socks, so she pulled those off too. She posed for him wearing nothing but a black lace bra and thong.

Grabbing her by the waist, Elson launched Kim onto his messy bed. He took hold of her waist, pulling her right to the edge of the mattress and falling to his knees between her spread thighs.

"Oh my god." She watched him target her pussy. His breath was so hot she could feel it through her thong. "Oh fuck, Elson, you gotta lick me."

He didn't even move her thong aside before planting his face in her crotch. Growling, he sucked there until his hot mouth soaked through the cotton lining. She'd never seen him so wild, biting her pussy lips or tearing at her thong with his teeth, shaking his head side to side. It was like watching an animal slashing into its prey. She was his gazelle. He could tear her to shreds, and she'd just keep calling out for more.

Waves of tingling heat coursed between her inner thighs as she wrapped them around Elson's head. He grabbed her bare ass, squeezing with both hands, but her muscles flexed each time she bucked, smashing her pussy against his face. She wanted more. Oh god, she wanted so much more.

Reaching between her legs, Kim tugged her thong to one side. The second Elson's tongue met her bare lips, Kim groaned. This agony was bliss. God, when he attacked her pussy like that she didn't feel in control of her mind or her body. He'd only just started and already she was bouncing on the bed, throwing herself at his mouth.

Kim couldn't tell Elson's saliva from her pussy juice—all she knew was she was wet. Damn wet. She thrust against his face, riding his mouth, feeling the prickle of his stubble against her baby-soft lips.

"I shaved for you!" She didn't mean to holler, but she couldn't help it.

Elson made a sound like "I know," or maybe "I noticed." Hard to tell exactly what he was saying with his mouth wide open and tongue extended like that. Everything sounded like a moan.

Pulling down the cup of her bra, Kim pinched her hard nipple and a shock wave went straight to her clit. She bucked even higher and Elson went with her, rising until he was standing next to the bed, holding her on a steep diagonal. The view made her gasp. He shook his head side to side, sucking her clit all the while.

An impatient orgasm throbbed at the base of her belly, seeping into her clit with every clench and gasp. She could feel her body more intensely than ever. Her skin blazed inside and out, and she wanted to scratch everywhere, even knowing it would do her no good. The only cure for this sizzle was pulsing in her pussy, begging for release.

"Make me come." It was hard to move in this position, but that didn't stop Kim grinding against his mouth. "Get me there, Elson. I want it now!"

Just as Kim squeezed her straining nipple, Elson sucked her clit into his mouth so hard she screamed. He buried his face in her pussy lips, going berserk between her legs. He put her over the brink so hard she didn't know what hit her.

Kim's orgasm trembled through her entire body. Her toes curled until they felt numb. She held her legs straight and still in an attempt to hold on to the sensation. But as fast as her climax had peaked, the pleasure grew too big to bear. She pounded her fists on the mattress, trying to flip herself over so he'd have to let go, but nothing worked.

Screaming, "Stop! Stop!" she flailed her arms, trying desperately to escape. Why was he still going at her, still sucking her aching clit? "No, Elson, stop! Stop!"

Something new.

This is what she'd asked for: *eat my pussy until I can't breathe—and then eat it some more.* If she could catch her breath, she might even laugh. But she was beyond screaming now, beyond pleading. For the first time ever, she'd passed her pain point and it hadn't killed her.

Kim went limp and Elson followed her onto the bed, his mouth still latched to her pussy. She let go of her thong and it stayed there, stuck between her thigh and her red mound. Her clit was so engorged it stuck out between her slick lips, and when Elson looked up at her, his face was wet with her juices.

For a moment, they just looked at each other. There was awe

in his eyes, and she felt the same way. And then he went right back at it, licking her clit, eating her like dinner. She didn't last a minute before another orgasm soared through her body. This one made her shake all over, made her buck and bounce on the bed, and forced a string of naughty words from her mouth. She clawed the sheets until every bit of energy was drained by her climax. She couldn't even see straight.

With an animal growl, Elson flipped her over and spanked her ass. It was so unexpected she tensed and whipped her head around. His smile was ruthless, and she loved it. She had absolutely no force left. It was all him now.

Elson rained spankings down on her ass. She was too orgasm-stupid to keep count, but it felt like a lot. They just kept coming, these raw smacks and slaps, until her skin sizzled. When her eyes focused, she saw how red her cheeks had become and felt like she'd swallowed wool. Every spanking was torture now. They were all so damn hard that she tried to roll over, but he wouldn't have it. He kneeled on her thighs to keep her in place. She turned to one side and the other, but there was no escape. He had her good.

"No, stop! Stop!" Kim squealed as tears formed in her eyes. She blinked, and those tears spread across her lashes. The whole room sparkled, but the spanking didn't stop.

"Something new." Elson's voice was dark, but regulated. "Like we said—eat you breathless, then eat you some more."

It hurt so much, and it was real pain, genuine and intense. She tried to squirm away, but he wouldn't let her move. Every slap was another slice of hell. She flinched when he raised his hand and howled when he lowered it, screamed when his palm struck her blazing flesh. She was crying now, honest-to-god tears, and no pain had ever felt this good.

"I said I'd spank you raw."

"Mission accomplished," she bawled, her breath hitching with every sob.

There was no hesitation in his actions as he climbed off her. Sure she was free to move, but damned if she had the energy for it now. When he pulled her to the edge of the mattress, she let her body slide against the mess of covers.

"What if I fuck you?"

All Kim could manage was a whispered, "Yesss."

Her toes met the floor, but she didn't stand. She couldn't. She lay there, facedown on Elson's bed, legs spread for him, hoping he'd get inside her soon. Damn soon.

When his fat cock penetrated her, it was too much and not enough. Something deep inside of her panged, and she clenched her pussy muscles, making him groan. He grabbed her waist hard, pulling her into the saddle of his hips. She made herself a toy for his pleasure, a rag doll. All her energy had been taken by force, by orgasms and spankings, and now she was a body of bliss.

Every time her searing ass met Elson's pelvis, she whimpered. Her flesh prickled with heat. As his thumbs moved down her rear, pressing into her cheeks on both sides, she muttered a litany of obscenities, blurred together by sensation and emotion. "Fuckmefuckmejustfuckme!"

He did. He fucked her so hard she felt it in her toes. Her body buzzed and a familiar sensation reappeared in her belly. "Holy fuck, I'm gonna fucking come!"

"You come!" Elson commanded, thrusting so fast it made her weak.

"I'm gonna fucking come!" she cried, like saying it again made it even more true.

There was something about Elson's voice, about the way he breathed and wheezed and grunted and growled, that she felt in her body. Her thighs were on fire from the inside out, and her pussy groped him, milked him, begged him to come. God, did he ever!

"Fuck yeah!" Elson rammed her robotically, like some mechanical force was driving his hips.

When Kim closed her eyes, the last of her tears spilled onto Elson's sheets. She could just see the come exploding from his cock and filling her pussy. She could see his white coating her pink, and the thought made her moan.

Kim didn't move when Elson collapsed beside her. Breath eluded them. Words did too. Even later, when Elson got under the covers, she had to stay on top. Her ass was still blazing.

"You really did a number on me." She kissed his cheek. "Thanks."

"So, was that something new?"

She laughed. "You bet."

"Thinking of moving in with me now?"

She took a breath, gazing up at the car poster above his bed. "There ain't enough room in this apartment for the two of us."

This time, he laughed. "Would you at least consider spending a few nights here? With me? Hmm?"

Elson looked so cute when he begged, and Kim couldn't help smiling. "After sex like that, how can I say no?"

OVER A BARREL

Tamsin Flowers

Bonnie Bryant hated winter weather. Even before she skidded on a patch of sidewalk ice and broke both her wrists the week after Thanksgiving. Not one wrist, like the old ladies who're unsteady on their feet or the kids who are running too fast to avoid a snowball, but two. Both her arms were in plaster from the wrist to the elbow. Now she didn't have to go out in the snow, but she had cabin fever and her mom's chicken soup to contend with instead.

In short, she was miserable and feeling sorry for herself. And frustrated. There are certain things you can't do with plaster casts on both your wrists.

"Come on, Bonnie. View it as a well-earned break from work," said her mother, ramming a sofa cushion down behind her daughter's back. "God knows, you worked enough hours overtime before Thanksgiving."

"Mom, I can't afford to take time off work. There are people in the office who would kill for my job and they're probably already warming up my seat."

"Don't be ridiculous," said Melba Bryant.

She was too busy and Bonnie found it exhausting to watch her scurrying around the living room, putting things away in the wrong place and tidying what didn't need to be tidied. She closed her eyes and wriggled on the cushions to try and make herself more comfortable.

"Right, I'm done."

Melba's voice from somewhere behind the couch cut through to her consciousness. She must have dozed off.

"I'm away now. I've left cut up sandwiches on the table for your lunch and I'll be back at six to sort dinner. Anything you need from the store?"

"No, Mom."

Bonnie shook her head sleepily, but then she remembered.

"Mom? Will you put the key out for me, please? Jason Haynes from the office is dropping by later to go over some files."

Melba came round to the front of the couch.

"For the love of god, why won't they leave you in peace? Well, at least this guy can tell you who's after your job."

"It's him, Mom. He's the one after my job."

When the key turned in the lock at a quarter after four Bonnie was watching an episode of *Dexter* she'd missed earlier in the run. She scrabbled for the remote, which dropped with a clatter to the floor and skidded under the couch. As Dexter pierced his victim's heart with a stiletto, Jason Haynes walked into the room and dropped his attaché case noisily on Bonnie's dining table.

"Not disturbing you, am I, Bonnie?" he said, as he shrugged out of a sharply cut black coat flecked white with snow.

"I was just switching off," said Bonnie, pointing toward where the remote fell. "Would you mind?"

Her cheeks burned. She hated Jason Haynes and hated the idea of him coming to her apartment. But the boss had left her with no choice. Jason needed information to complete some of her tasks and there was no way she was venturing back onto those icy sidewalks with both arms in plaster.

Jason bent down and retrieved the remote, silencing the gruesome noises coming from the television.

"Good to see you're finding useful ways to fill the days," he said.

Bonnie scowled but she knew better than to dig herself into a hole by trying to justify her viewing choice.

"Okay, Jason, let's get on with it," she said.

He nodded and she watched him as he moved one of her dining chairs closer to the couch and retrieved his case. His jet-black hair, always so perfect in the office, was a little wind-ruffled and speckled with rapidly melting snow, and his clean-shaved cheeks were rosy with cold. But other than that, and a slight water mark on one of his shoes, he was his usual pristine self. His charcoal suit was too expensive to show a crease and his shirt-tie combination was, as ever, in relentless good taste. How did he afford to dress so well given they were both doing the same job? Bonnie felt positively dowdy, slumped on the couch in her sweats.

He pulled a pile of folders out of his case and settled on the chair.

Bonnie sat forward on the couch and tried to feign interest. God, this was awkward.

"You want coffee?" she said. "Sorry, I should have suggested it before you sat."

"I've gotta make my own, right?" he said with a wry smile.

"'fraid so," Bonnie said apologetically.

"I bet you could do with one?"

"Only if you're…"

"Show me where everything is, and I'll make you the best cup you've had all day."

"Easy," laughed Bonnie, "Seeing as you're only in competition with my mom."

The ice was broken, so to speak, but once they were seated again, albeit with great coffee, Jason was all business. He opened the first file on his lap and pulled out a tender document Bonnie recognized. All those hours of slaving before Thanksgiving, distilled into four sheets of paper.

"The Bertram tender?" she said. "How's it going?"

"Look, Bonnie, I had to put off submitting it."

"What the fuck? It was supposed to go out the day I fell. It was all ready."

"I was going to send it off but then I gave it a quick read-through, just for typos."

"And?"

"And you'd made some pretty basic mistakes in your calculations."

Bonnie couldn't believe what she was hearing.

"Jason, I went through those figures half a dozen times. There were no mistakes. And Walter approved them."

Walter Brown was their mutual boss.

"There were mistakes, Bonnie."

Jason's tone brooked no argument, but that was exactly what he was going to get.

"Who do you think you are, coming in here and acting like the boss when, in fact, we're both at the same level and I've been working for the company longer?"

She'd been doing these tenders for years; he'd probably missed a stage out of the calculation and then assumed it was her error. But Jason didn't rise to the bait.

"I went over it with Walter and he agreed with me," he said calmly. "I submitted the new version this morning."

"Jesus, Jason, you can't do that. Bertram Brothers is my client."

"Bonnie, we work for the same company, for fuck's sake. They're all *our* clients. You messed up and I got it sorted. Don't be angry with me for saving your ass."

"Saving my ass! Yeah, and I wonder how Walter views it."

"If you don't like what's going on in the office without you, might I suggest you hurry on back?"

Bonnie was furious, furious enough to take a swing at him with one of her casts. But luckily for Jason, he was saved by the bell. Bonnie's cell phone sounded the klaxon that indicated her mother was on the line and, still glaring at Jason, she picked up.

"Mom, I can't talk now, I'm in a meeting."

"With the man who wants your job, right?"

This topic of conversation had to be right off-limits, with Jason sitting opposite her, surveying her apartment while he waited for her to finish.

"Mom!"

"Bonnie, it's important. It's the car. I can't get it to start and your father thinks the carburetor's gone, whatever that is. But basically I'm not going to be able to get over to do your dinner."

"Shit! Sorry, Mom. When do you think you'll be able to get here next?"

"I'll let you know. You better call a friend."

Bonnie dropped the cell phone on the couch with a sigh. Jason had obviously been all ears.

"Problem?"

"Evidently," snapped Bonnie. Jason was not the person in whom she wanted to confide her domestic problems. And damn him for sitting there looking so cool, calm and collected—not to mention bloody handsome—as she got more and more flustered.

"Bonnie, I was only going to check if you needed any help with things," said Jason, "but obviously you don't."

"That's right, Jason, I don't. Now, if we're done?"

"We're not." Jason pulled another file from his pile. "Walter wanted me to talk to you about a new tender, for a new client. He thought your input would be useful."

"Really?"

"Bonnie, grow up. I'm not out to take your job or steal your next promotion. Let's go through this tender and make it the best we can and then, seeing as your mom can't come, I'll make your dinner before I go."

And as if to make peace with her, he smiled at her. The full-megawatt Jason Haynes smile; the one that made her stomach flip even as she glared back at him. She bit back the sarcastic reply on the tip of her tongue.

"Thanks, Jason. Her car won't start, and I'm pretty useless on my own with these." She held up her two casts in an apologetic gesture.

Jason was as good as his word. They worked on the tender for an hour and Bonnie had to grudgingly admit to herself he knew what he was talking about. The result was better than anything she could have produced on her own. When they finished, Jason stashed all the files back into his attaché case.

"Now I'm starving," he said. "Is there enough for two?"

This couldn't have surprised Bonnie more. In the three months they had been working together they hadn't so much as shared a cup of coffee let alone a meal together.

"I don't know what Mom was going to cook but there's always pasta and tomatoes and bacon, if you can do something with those?"

Jason headed for the kitchen and Bonnie struggled up from

the couch to follow him. If she couldn't cook, the least she could do was tell him where everything was. She perched herself on a stool at the breakfast bar, letting the weight of her casts rest on the counter.

"Wine?" said Jason.

"There's a bottle of white in the fridge," said Bonnie. "Glasses are over in that top cupboard, and you'll find a corkscrew in the drawer."

Minutes later Jason had the bottle open and Bonnie was listening to the familiar *glug-glug-glug* of wine being poured. He held out a glass to her.

"I can't hold it," she said.

"Got any straws?"

When she shook her head, Jason came round to her side of the breakfast bar and slowly raised the glass up to her lips. She took a sip and, when he tilted it again, a large gulp.

"Thanks. That's the first mouthful of wine I've had since the accident and, boy, does it taste good."

Jason laughed and gave her another sip. Then he turned his attention to chopping onions and tomatoes to make a sauce for the pasta.

"What else have you been missing since you've had those things on your arms?" he said as they sat opposite each other at the dining table thirty minutes later, large dishes of pasta steaming in front of them.

He'd been most attentive throughout the cooking process, and Bonnie was on to a second glass of wine.

"Taking a bath," she said. "I have to go in the shower with plastic bags on my arms and mom has to help me wash my hair. It's humiliating, like being a little kid again."

"You don't like people looking after you, do you, Bonnie? You'd rather do it all on your own."

He saw she was struggling to get the spaghetti onto her fork.

"Here, let me," he said, shuffling his chair around to her side of the table.

"Nobody likes to be babied," she said.

He gave her another mouthful of wine and then fed her some pasta. Bonnie wondered if she was getting a little drunk but it was such a pleasant change from the finger food her mom had been preparing that she didn't care.

"Oh, I don't know," said Jason. "It's nice to let someone else take the strain, from time to time."

He swept a stray lock of hair back from her forehead and tucked it behind her ear. It was a totally natural gesture, with no self-consciousness at all. It made Bonnie wonder if he'd had experience in looking after invalids.

"So I suppose you can't get dressed or undressed on your own, either?"

Bonnie felt her face flame red. It seemed like such a silly thing to get coy about, given the circumstances, but suddenly all she could think about was Jason's tanned and sculpted hands removing her clothing. All of it.

"I don't need any help from you, if that's what you were offering."

She heard his sharp intake of breath at the idea of it. It was time Jason Haynes got going. But he obviously didn't think so; he topped her glass up with wine and held it to her mouth.

"No, Jason, I've had enough."

He immediately put the glass down.

"Sorry if my behavior's been a little crass," he said, with a shrug of his shoulders. "Is there anything else I can do for you before I go?"

With a rush of heat between her legs, Bonnie suddenly knew

exactly what she'd like Jason to do for her. She could hardly believe what she was thinking, but then these bloody casts meant she'd had to go two weeks already without an orgasm. It wasn't exactly the kind of thing you could ask your mom to do for you.

"Bonnie?" Jason's voice cut into her thoughts like a knife into butter. "What is it?"

Bonnie shook her head but her face flushed with embarrassment. Again.

"I'm fine, Jason. Thanks for everything you've done."

Jason got up and carried their empty plates back to the kitchen.

"When d'you think you'll be back in the office?"

Bonnie shrugged. "As soon as these are off."

"We're missing you." Jason took a step toward her. "Correction. I'm missing you."

Without thinking, Bonnie stepped in to meet him. He put his hands on her shoulders and his dark, sultry eyes locked on to hers. It seemed a little surreal for him to say he was missing her at work and to now be standing in what certainly qualified as each other's personal space.

"Bonnie..." His voice sounded an octave lower than usual.

Thinking about it afterward, Bonnie never knew what possessed her to do as she did next. Perhaps it was the sexual frustration brought about by two weeks in plaster casts or perhaps it was the proximity of a good-looking man in a small space after half a bottle of wine. She tilted her face upward, raised herself on her toes and stretched forward until her lips just brushed against his. Her casts were too unwieldy for her to put her arms around his neck; they hung limp at her side.

For a split second, she thought that was it. He didn't respond and she wondered if she'd misheard what he'd said about missing her. Her heart was racing and she took a deep breath, but the intoxicating smell of him made things worse rather than better. She knew she should step back and apologize but she was too unsure of her legs to move.

Then, as if waking from a trance, Jason did respond. His arms wrapped around her waist, pulling her body tight against his, and his mouth took possession of hers. There was nothing tentative about this kiss. His lips encircled hers and before she realized what was happening his tongue had pushed its way into her mouth. Desire surged up through her belly and she pushed her tongue against his in return. As her legs turned to water, she pressed her hips against his; she could feel the growing bulge in his pants pressing against her stomach.

Bonnie would have been fooling herself if she'd pretended she hadn't imagined kissing Jason in a variety of office situations. But she'd never for one minute thought her fantasies would come to pass. Let alone in her own apartment.

But, abruptly, he pushed her away and took a step back.

"What?" said Bonnie. Her voice didn't sound like her own.

"This is wrong," said Jason. "I feel like I'm taking advantage of your situation."

It felt like a kick in the guts to Bonnie. For some reason he'd changed his mind.

"Jason, I'm not some damsel in distress," she said. "Remember who started it?"

"I know…" he said. "But what about when you come back to work?"

"We'll have to cross that bridge when we come to it."

Brave words, but she was feeling anything but sure of herself. This could be the biggest mistake ever. But she really needed to feel Jason's hands on her skin and his mouth…dammit, she needed to feel his mouth on her pussy.

He stared at her, wide eyed, breathing heavily through slack lips.

"You can't leave now," she said. She felt so vulnerable, making her need for him so obvious. He was her coworker and not only that, he was also her biggest rival in the office. What the hell was she playing at?

"God, Bonnie..." It was more of a moan than coherent words.

He stepped forward and swept her up in his arms.

"Bedroom?"

"Through there."

She waved one of her casts in the direction of her room.

There was no stopping them now; it was as if the floodgates had opened. Jason pushed open the bedroom door with his foot and deposited her on the bed. She lay and watched as he pulled his shirt out of his pants, unknotted his tie and started frantically undoing his shirt buttons. When he got to the fastening of his pants, she let out a whimper, and then he was in front of her in all his naked glory, with one of the finest cocks she'd ever seen standing proudly to attention. Her mouth was dry but her pussy was immediately wet. She kicked her shoes off but other than that, she was at Jason's mercy when it came to getting naked too.

He didn't make her wait. As quickly as he'd undressed himself, he pulled off the sweatpants and T-shirt she'd been wearing for the sake of ease and comfort. All she had on was a pair of blush silk panties; she hadn't been able to face the indignity of asking Melba to do her bra up.

"My beautiful Bonnie," Jason whispered, and he leant down to catch one of her dusky nipples between his teeth.

Bonnie moaned; it was like a current passing through her, all the more intense for having lain dormant for so long. She hadn't been able to touch herself, and now she was desperate to touch Jason. But the two casts effectively immobilized her arms. She lay back with the plasters reaching above her head on the pillow, making her feel like a sacrificial offering for Jason to do with what he wanted. His fuck toy. It made her feel hornier than ever.

Jason switched his attention to her other breast, nipping it sharply and twisting it between his fingers and thumb. Bonnie's hips bucked with the flash of pain, a move that seemed to remind Jason there were other areas still to be explored. He knelt up between her legs, gazing down at her. Then, very slowly, he pushed her silky panties down over her hips. As they pulled away from between her legs, Bonnie felt a trail of warm juices dragging down her thigh, wetting her leg. Jason tossed the panties to one side and with a swift flick of his wrists splayed her legs wide.

"Beautiful," he murmured, reaching out with one hand to touch the part of Bonnie that had felt most neglected.

As she felt his palm cup the front of her pussy, Bonnie groaned.

"You've been needing this, haven't you, Bonnie?" said Jason.

His fingers glided easily down the cleft between her labia and pushed deep inside her with a fast, hard thrust. Bonnie yelped at the sensation that flared up through her body and then pushed her hips up to meet him.

"Yes, I've been needing this," she said through gritted teeth. "Now, Jason, I need you inside me now."

"Condom?"

"In the drawer," she said.

It was one of her favorite things, rolling a condom down her lover's cock, but this time she had to leave it up to Jason. He ripped the package open and it literally made her mouth water to see him carefully roll it on.

He didn't waste any more time. With one hand he guided his cock to the mouth of her pussy and then, sitting back on his heels, he pulled her hips up until he had her impaled. He started thrusting, gripping her hips hard, his fingers digging into her flesh, and Bonnie's shoulders were pulled down the bed with each plunge as her hips were raised higher.

His cock was long and the position enabled him to push it deep inside her. Bonnie felt as if she would be split in two, but it was a feeling she'd been needing for so long. He lowered her hips and leaned forward, pushing harder and faster, and Bonnie raised her legs around his waist. She didn't think he could go any farther into her but he did and each thrust forced a grunt from the back of her throat. His mouth found first one nipple, then the other, and he pushed one hand down between them to find her clit.

The moment his finger swept around her most sensitive spot was liftoff for Bonnie. The orgasm that unfurled within her grew and grew, sweeping every sensation in its path, taking away her sense of place, of time and even of self. Her back arched beneath him, and her hips opened wider than ever. Her muscles clenched as if they wanted to hold his cock there forever and as they pulsed around him, she felt him stiffen in response. With a roar he came, grasping her tightly to him as he emptied himself, remaining pulsating inside her as his orgasm subsided.

They were both drenched in sweat when he flopped down on her chest and she could feel his softening cock slipping out of her.

"Jesus, Bonnie, how good's it going to be when you can use your hands as well?" he said breathily in her ear.

She laughed.

"When I get my hands back, do you think I'll need you?"

"Say you will, baby," he said.

"It might cost you dinner... And you'll have to stop pointing out my shortcomings to Walter."

"I promise, Bonnie, from now on, Walter's only gonna hear good things about you."

"Just as long as you don't tell him too much..."

"To ensure which, you'll have to keep me happy."

"Well, Mr. Haynes, we seem to have each other over a barrel."

"Couldn't think of a better place to have you."

And as he kissed her, Bonnie had the pleasingly graphic image in her mind of Jason Haynes taking her over a barrel. And wondered where she could get one...

TUSCARORA

Anja Vikarma

Jane began to climb the hill. As she crunched through last season's fallen leaves, each footstep said, *Yes, yes, yes*. She felt the *yes* move up her legs, buoying her gait, filling her with a happiness she didn't know she could feel. It was a light feeling, a hopeful feeling, a new feeling.

The land beneath her feet was hers. An unexpected windfall from a distant uncle, now deceased. The land beneath her feet had provided the escape she would need from a life she had stumbled into at too young an age. Jane had received the news, told the bad husband to kiss her ass, packed her belongings and moved from the Big Apple to the acreage upstate.

She now possessed a farmhouse full of an impressive variety of junk, a meadow that deer passed through each morning and evening, and a hillside of woods. On the map, she could see a wide stream, Tuscarora Creek, passing through the land on the other side of the hill, and that was her destination for the afternoon.

She continued her climb with the sun at her back. The temperature increased and sweat began to dribble down her spine as she picked her way around tree roots and rocks. She crested the hill and began to descend, listening to blue jays yak about her presence and smelling a damp earthiness that was new to her. Nothing in the city smelled so rich and full of potential. It enlivened her, as if her body had known all its life it belonged here. She smiled.

Jai Ganesha, she thought. A quick honor to the elephant-headed deity that she had met in her yoga class. "He is the remover of obstacles," the leader of the kirtan chanting class had told them before leading the group through many minutes of *Jai Ganesha* and *Om Gum Ganapateya Namaha.*

Jane had latched on to the idea of a supernatural power removing obstacles and had spent the better part of the past year humming, "*Jai Ganesha. Om Gum Ganapateya Namaha,*" under her breath. When the bad husband was in his best bad-husband mode, the words rolled through her head, blocking out his hurtful words. She had taken great comfort, knowing a way out was opening before her. When the package from the lawyer had arrived, she immediately sat down and sent a check to the Elephant Sanctuary, writing *Jai Ganesha* on the note line of the check. It was her way of saying, "Thank you! Thank you! Thank you!"

She heard the stream before she saw it. Smelled the wet, shale rock—a flinty smell that tickled her nostrils. The forest came to an abrupt end at a ledge about four feet above Tuscarora Creek. Damp, moss-covered rocks enticed her to step down and get closer. Sunlight bounced off the water, winking at her playfully, inviting her in. She climbed down, pulled off her sneaker, and dipped her foot in the sparkling stream.

"Oh!" she exclaimed.

In spite of the heat of the early summer sun, the water still carried the cold of spring. Jane looked across the stream and saw a large ledge of flat rock hovering over the cool water. Heat shimmered off its dark surface, inviting her to come sit a spell. She pulled off her other shoe and picked her way across the stream, enjoying the cool caress on her calves.

She settled crossed-legged—easy pose, her yoga teacher called it—on the warm rock, closed her eyes, and pictured Ganesh in her mind. Quietly, she chanted "*Jai Ganesha,*" and the stream happily sang along. With her face to the sun, Jane felt the last remnants of the bad husband sink from her. The rock felt strong and steady enough to hold those memories. She could let them go.

"*Om Shanti, Shanti, Shanti, Om,*" she began to chant. Peace, peace, peace. Her voice warmed as the words permeated her heart. She sang louder, rocking gently. The creek warbled along with her, a wonderful harmony she had never experienced in class. "*Om, Shanti, Shanti, Shanti, Om.*"

"Will that attract fish?"

The man's voice startled her from her mediation. Her legs popped out of easy pose, her hand flew to her heart and she almost fell into the creek. The Tuscarora laughed, and it sounded like a brew of mirth and sunlight.

The man stood to her left, holding a fishing pole and grinning down at her. Jane scrambled to her feet, straightened her shirt and smoothed back her hair. "Pardon me?"

He cocked his thumb back over his shoulder and said, "I was downstream, wondering why I couldn't get a bite today, when I heard this sound, singing—like the water nymphs were teasing my fish away."

"Hardly. Mostly teasing away bad memories," she said.

Under his ball cap, Jane could see kind brown eyes flecked with gold. A smile lurked around the corners of his wonderfully full lips. Jane thought, *Although kissing those lips could chase memories away too.* The unbidden thought shocked her. She had been sure she wouldn't want anything to do with a man for a least a decade.

He pushed his cap back, swiped the back of his hand across his forehead and pulled the brim back down. "Well, you sounded like a water nymph to me. It was lovely. That said..." he smiled broadly, "you're trespassing on my land. Care to introduce yourself?"

Jane looked down at the rock beneath her feet, as if expecting to see PROPERTY OF... written there. She looked back up at his bewitching smile. "Jane Harmony. I live just over the hill."

"For real? The singing nymph's name is Harmony?"

She rolled her eyes. "Please don't call me a nymph."

"Okay. Sorry. I just really enjoyed the sound of your voice."

Jane wondered if she should tell him that "Harmony" was a name she'd given herself. Her maiden name was a Polish nightmare of consonants, and her married name tasted like ash in her mouth. With her opportunity to start afresh, she gifted herself a name that exemplified what she thought her life should become.

He extended his hand. "Beauregard Bradford, but as you might guess, people call me Beau."

She shook his hand, her palm tingling under his touch. "Sorry about trespassing. It's just, well, you've got the sunshine on your side of the creek."

"True."

"Is it okay if I sit awhile longer?"

"Come sit everyday if you'd like. Sing too. What were you singing, by the way?"

She scuffed her toe on the rock, feeling slightly silly. "Uh, it's called kirtan. It's Hindu chanting."

"Uh-oh." A look of concern crossed his face.

"What?"

"Hindu, huh? A heathen among us."

"Heathen!" Her mouth dropped open.

"You're in the boonies, baby. Folks are gonna wonder about John Kleszczynska's kin being Hindu." He laughed, and Jane grew slightly irritated.

"I didn't say I was Hindu, I said I was chanting kirtan."

He reached out and briefly touched her shoulder. "Hey! No problem by me. Just giving you fair warning about life in the boonies. You sound like a city girl, and that will be strike one against you. Chanting Hindu-like will be strike two."

She put her hands on her hips and narrowed her eyes. "And what will be strike three, do you suppose?"

He worked the brim of his cap up and down a few times, thinking. "Taking up with that nice Bradford boy, perhaps?"

She dropped her arms, flummoxed by the rush of heat that leaped up from a deep place, set her heart thumping and caused what was sure to be a bright, pink blush to bloom across her cheeks. She turned her face toward Tuscarora Creek, as if the creek would supply her with an appropriately glib reply.

He laughed. Jane, despite her flustered state, noted the way his laugh seemed to blend harmoniously with the chuckling of the creek. "Hey, I'm kidding," he said. "We just met and I'm a good, Christian country boy."

She looked back at his delightful grin, broad shoulders and trim hips. Her nipples began to harden with approval, so she quickly crossed her arms across her chest. She rolled her eyes again and said, "Oh, I bet."

He touched his hand to the edge of his hat and said, "Look, it was great to meet you, Miss Harmony. Sit as long as you'd like. I'm fishing again Thursday, so do me a favor and use your nymph-like voice to sing the fish down to that bend, there." He gestured downstream. And with that he turned, hopped up the bank and disappeared into the tangle of willows and scrub.

Jane stared into the greenery awhile, replaying the whole encounter in her mind a few times over, marveling that a part of her, the part of her that she'd been sure the bad husband had starved to death, was alive and well and eagerly anticipating Thursday.

Wednesday flew by as Jane hauled three more loads of Uncle John's junk to the county transfer station. She fell in bed exhausted. But the flicker in her belly, the source of her blush, was wide awake and perpetually sending her images of Beau Bradford: his smile, his laugh, the shape of him. The flicker enticed her hand to caress the skin of her abdomen, her hip, her thigh. Her wandering hand traveled up and down and...

"Stop it," she whispered to herself, and shoved her hand under the pillow.

Jane fell asleep making a list of why it would be a bad idea to take up with her neighbor so soon after cutting the bad husband out of her life. As she drifted off, she thought she could hear the flicker in her belly and the burbling of Tuscarora Creek whispering, conspiring. She dreamed of crossing the creek on the back of a purple elephant, but woke before she found out where it was taking her.

Thursday morning she attempted to make sense of her uncle's gardening journal, thumbed through old seed catalogs, and walked about the fenced-in, weed-infested plot of land behind the house. Jane had never grown so much as a strawberry and had no idea where to begin. But ever since discovering the lusciousness of fresh strawberries at the farm stand three miles from her house, strawberries had been her motivation to learn to garden.

Jane knew the dirt needed to be turned if any seeds were to make it into the soil. She worked through the lunch hour, leaning on the spade, lifting and turning the dark earth. The bad husband had told her she would hate living alone. But each earthworm and toad she discovered, each bouncing robin warbling at her progress, made it clear to her that she was anything but alone. She was sharing her new home with hundreds, if not thousands of other living creatures. A contented smile danced on her face, and contemplating her new companions helped her ignore the spade-induced ache in her thighs and back.

Thursday afternoon she headed up and over the hill, sweating even more than last time, as the humidity had risen. Thick clouds lumbered across the summer sky while carnal thoughts skipped across her consciousness. She frowned at the clouds and swatted the thoughts away as quickly as they rose. "I just want to see the creek again," she told the scolding blue jays. They didn't believe her.

When she reached Tuscarora Creek, she felt relief rather than shock at the cold water. She waded across and climbed on to the large rock outcropping. She glanced up and down the creek, but her neighbor was nowhere to be seen. Sitting in easy pose for a bit, "*Om, Shanti, Shanti, Shanti, Om*" rhythmically passed her lips. Rhythmic, at least, until a tremendous yawn interrupted the flow.

Her legs, fatigued from the spading, grew achy in easy pose. She lay back, stretching out full across the rock, and watched the large, white cumulonimbus clouds wander across the blue sky. She didn't remember closing her eyes. She didn't remember hearing anyone or anything approach her. But she never forgot what she heard next.

"Jane," he whispered. Her belly jumped, remembering his voice.

"Miss Harmony, don't move." His voice was so close that the breeze of his words roused her more than their meaning.

"Wha…" she began to turn toward him.

His hand clamped down on her shoulder. "Don't move. There's a rattler next to you."

He was squatting down beside her, but his eyes were fixed somewhere over her right shoulder.

"What?" She blinked rapidly, trying to process what he'd said.

He looked down at her and flashed a quick smile. "Don't panic, but there is a rattlesnake sunning itself about five inches to your right."

Jane felt her blood turn as cold as the creek's water. The bad husband had told her about all the things she was sure to hate about living in the country: the bugs, the bats, the mud, the bears and, of course, the snakes. The snakes had been the only truly worrisome item on his list.

A weird sound squeaked out of her throat. She searched Beau's face. Would he kill it? A new feeling rose up. The snake was her new neighbor too. She didn't want it dead. "What do I do?" she whispered.

He wrapped his hand firmly around her forearm, "Grab my arm, like this. I'm going to pull you up so quick, Mr. Snake might not even know you've left."

They clasped forearms and he whispered "One, two…" and on "three," he rose quickly from his squat. She was pulled right along with him, pivoting away from the rock and toward his body.

"Whoa, whoa, whoa," he said as he began to backpedal.

"Oh god!" she shrieked, as she threw her other arm over his shoulder and flung her weight into him, wanting to get as far from the snake as she could.

The combined momentum sent them both backward into

Tuscarora Creek. He stumbled back; cold water splashed up around them. She glanced over her shoulder and saw the long, sinuous form. At the sight of the snake, Jane began to pedal her legs, as if she could climb her neighbor to safety. He completely lost his footing and they both went down into the chill, flowing waters of the creek.

He came up laughing. She sat waist deep in the water, staring at the rock, heart hammering, body shaking. He clasped her arm again and hoisted her back up.

"You okay?"

She turned away from the snake and threw her arms around his neck. "Oh my god! Oh my god. Sweet Jesus!"

"Oh, so you're a Christian after all," he laughed.

She pulled back to look at him wide eyed. "I...I..." Words failed her.

"Thank you?" he prompted.

She kissed him so hard they almost fell back into the creek. The Tuscarora seemed to chuckle approvingly.

Beau tightened his arms around her waist and kissed her back. Her breath quickened and when she opened her mouth slightly, her tongue surprised her by coming forward to meet his. Neither of them noticed the cold water around their knees; the heat building between them kept it at bay.

"Thank you, thank you, thank you," Jane said between kisses. When she felt his desire begin to rise against his shorts she realized what she was doing and pulled back. "Wow," she said simply.

He licked his lips and smiled, "Yeah, wow."

"Did you just save my life?" she asked.

He shrugged. "Maybe, maybe not. They're really more scared of you than you are of them."

Jane's short laugh wobbled. "Doubtful!"

He stooped and fetched a rock from the creek bottom. He tossed it gently, underhanded. The rock bounced twice across the ledge before bumping up against the rattlesnake. It jumped.

"See, he was as sound asleep as you."

The snake yawned—*I didn't know snakes yawned!* Jane thought—and slithered slowly from the ledge.

He put his hands back on her waist. "I shoulda thought to tell you about 'em on Tuesday. Hey," he looked down, "you're bleeding!"

Jane looked down and sure enough, both her kneecaps trickled rivulets of blood down her shins, briefly staining the water pink, and the Tuscarora carried it away. "Oh, gosh. Just what I need, more scars!"

"C'mon," he said, as he took her hand and began to lead her from the creek.

"Where are we going?"

"I've got a camper set up not far from here," he said.

Jane couldn't take her eyes from the ground as they walked. She didn't know if she would be able to take her eyes from the ground for a long time. As lovely as it was to have so many new, living creatures around her, snakes were ones she would rather avoid.

Beau led her into a small pop-up camper, sat her on the sleeping platform, and pulled a first-aid kit from under the sink. As he swabbed and bandaged her knees, he told her that the snakes were usually on the south-facing sides of the hill, and that it wouldn't be a bad idea to walk with a walking stick through the woods. "Let the stick shuffle the leaves ahead of you, not your foot," he said.

He finished applying the second Band-Aid, placed both his hands on her thighs and tenderly kissed each knee. He smiled up at her. "All better?"

Jane smiled. "All better," she said, and leaned down to kiss his forehead.

His hands squeezed her thighs gently, and when she pulled back, he followed. His face hovered above hers. "Miss Harmony, may I kiss you?"

She laughed. "We already kissed."

"You kissed me, you godless heathen. I was taught proper. I ask first!"

And then, without her reply, he kissed her deeply. So deeply Jane felt the heat of his kiss go down to her wounded knees and make them tingle. His hands, still on her thighs, squeezed again and her thighs began to tremble. Jane reached her arms around his waist and leaned back, pulling him over on top of her.

One of his hands left her thigh and slid slowly across her hip, along her waist and settled on her rib cage. He leaned back and looked down at her. "You're very fit," he said.

"Yoga," she said, and then pulled his lips back to hers. His hand continued upward, passed briefly across her breast and then stole up around the back of her neck. Her hand, in turn, ventured from his waist down to his rear end. She gave it a squeeze and then pulled back.

"You're very fit," she giggled.

"Farming," he said, and grabbed her by the shoulders. With one quick, strong move, he lifted her and slid her all the way back into the sleeping area. Her legs, as if by reflex, circled his waist.

Outside, the fat clouds began to rumble, as if sensing a great event had begun. The air around them grew hotter as their breath came quicker. His hands began to roam from her hair to her neck, her shoulder, to her waist. Jane felt safe under his slow, cautious progress. She also felt the size and shape of his erection pressing against her thigh. She lifted gently against him; in her mind, she was already enjoying the size of him within her.

He slid her shirt up and began to slide his hand back and forth across her flat stomach. He leaned back and glanced down. "Yoga? Really?"

"*Ashtanga* yoga," Jane clarified. "It's very physical."

"You're very physical," he said.

"I almost forgot I liked being physical."

She paused, hearing her own words and realizing just what the past years had cost her. The bad husband had been bad in so many ways. She reached for his neck and pulled him back down to her.

His hand slid under her bra and began to gently squeeze. One finger began to explore the hardness of her nipple. She kissed his neck. A wanting kiss. A hungry kiss. His other hand fumbled the button of her shorts loose and then he stopped.

"What?" she panted. She searched his face. "Did you just remember you're a good Christian boy?"

He laughed hard enough to rock his head back. "Hardly!" He kissed her stomach. "I was just thinking, we really should get you out of these wet clothes."

Outside, the gathered clouds began to push the wind through the trees, as if agreeing with him. Jane nodded mutely, and crossed her arms behind her head, watching Beau-the-neighbor pull off each shoe, toss her dripping socks into the sink and hook his fingers through the belt loops of her cutoff shorts. He began to tug, and she wiggled her hips to help his progress.

She sat up so he could pull the shirt from her head and helpfully reached back to undo the clasp of her bra. She leaned back on her elbows and watched his face as he looked her up and down. "God, you're beautiful," he whispered, and kissed her belly again.

"Hey!" she said, "What about your wet clothes?"

He kicked his shoes into the corner and had his shorts and T-shirt off almost before she finished the sentence. His cock now stared her right in the eye. Jane stared right back, then licked her lips and reached out to pull it toward her mouth. He groaned and held the ceiling of the camper for balance.

Jane liked the way his cock filled her mouth. Just enough, but not too much. She liked the smell of him. As her tongue roamed around the circumference of his cock, his smell made her think of fresh strawberries, and warm rocks and summer sun. Outside, the wind whistled and the leaves in the trees applauded her enthusiasm. Rain began to patter on the canvas walls.

She leaned back to smile up at him. "Sounds like we're getting a thunderstorm," she said.

As if on cue, the clouds let loose a long, low rumble, and the interior of the camper darkened by half. "We're getting something," he said in a low voice, and pushed her back. He lay across her and let his cock nudge up against her. The flicker in her belly was now a full, roaring fire, inviting him in.

The ache between her hips grew with want. The wind also intensified, and the camper trembled. Jane lifted one knee over his shoulder, hoping to encourage his entry. But he didn't enter. He slid back, lifted one hand up to hold her calf that had been on his shoulder, and began to kiss her stomach again. He kissed the slight protrusion of her hip bones—first right, then left. Jane moaned, and the wind outside moaned back. The camper shook again.

He kissed her inner thigh and then let his tongue begin a wandering journey. Jane writhed as his tongue dipped in, slid up, circled about, circled about, circled about. The camper brightened with sudden light, followed quickly by a thud of thunder.

He paused to look up at her. "It's very close," he said.

She nodded, closed her eyes and gently brought his head back down so his tongue could continue its delightful dance. Lightning flashed again; pleasure flashed through Jane. Thunder rolled, and she rolled her hips against him. The rain rose in tempo, and Jane's passion followed.

"It *is* getting close," she panted.

"I can tell," he said.

He kept his hand on her calf, keeping her one leg lifted high. He rose up, positioned himself and then slowly, as if he had all the time in the world, settled into her. He sunk in so deep that it pushed all thought and reason from her mind. Jane's cry was lost in a clap of thunder that seemed to slap the world away.

He began to draw back, paused deliciously and pushed slowly back into her as the rain began to lash the camper in its own passionate rhythm. Jane's head rocked side to side. She fell into a well of incredulous disbelief at the depth of her pleasure. He reached his other hand around, clasping one firm gluteal muscle and pulling her even tighter to him, even as she was meeting every thrust.

Jane relished the building energy in the center of herself. It almost felt sharp, intense as it was. The sharpness of it rose and rose and became almost unbearable. She heard her own voice over the wind and rain, "Yes! Yes! Yes!" It was as if the mantra of her feet two days prior had found a strong voice in her flaring desire. In the flashing light, she saw his face, mouth wide open, fixated on her as he filled her again and again.

His looking was so intense, almost hawk-like in its focus. She wanted his mouth on hers and pulled him down. Their kiss was woven with breath, and tongue and passion. The weight of him met her unbearable need, and she felt herself rising to a new place.

"So close, so close, so close," she was now panting under her breath.

He stayed true to his form, held his tempo and carried her above and beyond what she thought pleasure could be. It broke over her like water over rocks. It swept through her like wind through trees. Jane shuddered like a camper in a storm. From a distant place, she was aware that he too seemed to be breaking past a barrier, letting loose.

Jane floated on waves of utter release. They enveloped her, like living *Shanti*. Her body sighed from the inside out and the rain outside ebbed to a steady patter. The kettledrum thunder rolled over the next hill, as if telling the trees to the east what a great show they had missed. Beau rested his head on her shoulder.

"*Shanti, Shanti, Shanti,*" she whispered.

"What does that mean?" he murmured against her neck.

"Peace, Peace, Peace," she told him, and let her hand begin to wander up and down his back.

"Do you feel peaceful?"

"I have been at peace ever since I came here," she said. "There is something about this land that fits me."

"Except the snakes," he said, still directing his words to the space beneath her ear.

"Oh no," she said. "I've decided I love the snakes."

He lifted up and gave her a skeptical look. "How's that?"

She kissed him. "Wanting to see Tuscarora Creek brought me to you," she said, "But the snake brought you to me."

He laughed, and said, "I couldn't wait to get to you…snake or no snake."

"Even though I'm a heathen?"

"City girl, heathen and strike three…" he kissed her gently, "you've taken up with the Bradford boy."

Outside, dappled by the remaining raindrops, Tuscarora Creek burbled and laughed and carried their new story downstream.

BIG BULLY

A. M. Hartnett

It was my job to act out, or at least everyone seemed to think so. It was Teal's job to make sure I didn't go too far.

I was in the backseat of his car, his actual car and not the boring sedan he usually chauffeured me around in. I didn't know shit about cars, but Teal's personal ride was a slick red bullet that cornered like it was one with the road.

Not that I expected Teal to drive a shitty car. He worked his ass off for my father and was paid well. Of course, he would have his toys.

"I don't see why you have your thong in such a twist," I muttered under my breath.

He didn't answer me. Eyes on the road. I shifted the blanket around my shoulders. I'd only been damp when he'd showed up, but I was still freezing. Swimming in the Atlantic in mid-November will do that.

"Those were my friends," I went on to break the silence. "None of them would sell me out."

"*All* your friends would sell you out," he said.

"Is it so hard to believe anyone would just like me enough to keep their cameras in their purses?"

"Stop talking. You're slurring. You know how that gets on my nerves."

You'd swear from the way he talked to me I was the employee and he was the employer. No one talked to me like he did. I was accustomed to getting my way, and Teal was the only person who never let me get my way.

Teal had come into my life when I was eighteen, right after my first and only DUI. It was a stupid thing to do and my apology to my fans was genuine, but it put me on the list of former child stars spiraling out of control. I wasn't half as bad as the press made me out to be, I swear. I was drug free, but I didn't have the discipline to stop myself when I started drinking. It wasn't the booze, it was the letting go that booze let me do. This usually meant I ended up in embarrassing situations, even if they did seem like a good idea at the time.

Isn't that how it always goes?

Usually when I was having a bit of fun and Teal had to come collect me, he'd have to ram through a wall of photographers to get to me. It was something else to watch him. He'd grab me and just shoulder them out of the way like King Kong playing high-school football.

"So who tipped you off? You're the only one who showed up."

"One of your friends called the press. I have connections that make sure I get most calls first."

I didn't say anything as the sting went deep. I didn't really think those people were my friends. I had three friends I could count on. Everyone else was just an accessory or an employee, at least until they sold my location to the tabloids and got Teal on my ass.

Still, I preferred the illusion that my hangers-on adored me. I sure as hell didn't like Teal quipping about it.

I sucked in a breath and peered at him in the semidarkness. When he was first introduced to me he'd been a scary mountain of a man wedged inside a suit and tie, his head shaved and his gray eyes hard. He'd since grown out his salt-and-pepper hair and had abandoned his enforcer uniform for a less conspicuous jeans and T-shirt combination. It made him no less menacing.

Tonight he looked like a combination of his old self and new, matching the jeans with a button-up shirt and jacket over the top.

"You smell good," I said.

"I was on a date."

"Get the fuck out."

His look was poison. "My entire world doesn't revolve around pulling you out of your shit."

"So you just took off on her? Classy."

His mouth hardened, and he reached forward to turn on the radio.

Teal rarely took a night off, so I had taken advantage of his absence to get into some trouble. No one to stop me from doing those shots, no one to stop me from stripping down to my bra and panties for a swim, no one to stop me from being the bad girl.

The winking lights coming from the homes in the hills soon gave way to the incessant neon of the city. Thank god. My feet were like ice. I didn't dare ask Teal to turn the heat up. I sat in shivering silence until we reached our exit and he just drove on past.

"Shit," I said, sitting up. "You're not taking me to Dad's, are you? I don't think he'd be too happy if we knock on his door at three o'clock in the morning."

He shook his head. "I'm taking you to my place."

"Are you kidding me? Why?"

"Because it's my day off and I want my own fucking bed, that's why. You can be uncomfortable on my sofa for a change."

Wow.

I'd never heard him so pissed off before. If it was anyone else I would have flicked the diva switch and thrown a fit, but I knew from experience that it would never work on Teal. Nothing worked on Teal. I couldn't con him the way I had conned his predecessors.

"How many shots did you have tonight?"

I'll admit it: his tone was a little scary. "I don't know. *Lots*."

"So you had *lots* of tequila and decided it would be a smart move to jump in the ocean?"

"I guess."

"For fuck sake, Charlotte, at what point do you fucking grow up?"

I didn't want to cry in front of him, but I couldn't help it. My eyes burned with tears. I felt smaller and smaller, but I guess that was the point. His animosity was alive inside the car.

Sniffling, I turned to him. "I'm not as bad as I used to be, you know."

"Only because I'm around just about every waking hour."

Which was mostly true. I couldn't take too much credit for having kept my nose clean, especially not after proving I would get into shit the second I was out of Teal's clutches.

I stared down at my cold toes and shook my head. "I'm sorry I ruined your night."

It seemed to me as though he was working on his next words. He did this thing when he took a time out, pressing his lips together and twisting his mouth at the corners. It ended when he swiped his hand over his face and sighed. It was how he got rid of his anger and kept in control.

He didn't do it this time. He was going to remain pissed off.

When we rolled up to a stoplight, he met my gaze and held it. I couldn't tell whether it was the shadows or exhaustion, but I could see the years spent at my beck and call etched on his face.

Was it time, or had I done that to him?

The tension ended when the car behind us laid on the horn. Teal faced forward and shifted gears. The car rocketed forward. Neither of us said anything more for the rest of the ride.

I need to give up drinking, I thought, as we arrived at his condo and the underground parking swallowed us up. I didn't like how funny the booze had made me feel tonight.

His car rumbled as he swung into a spot marked with the number 934. I didn't make a move to get out after Teal did. I sat there until I realized he wasn't coming to open my door as usual. Leaving the blanket behind, I hopped out and rushed after him, bare feet slapping the concrete. The car chirped as he armed it.

I caught up with him at the elevator.

"You don't seem like a condo kind of guy, Teal," I said as we waited. "You seem like the survivalist type who has a camper down by the beach."

"There's a lot you don't know about me," he said, and I could have sworn he smiled a little.

It was impossible. Teal didn't smile. He scowled. He pinned your ass to the wall with that menacing stare.

My stomach lurched as the elevator shot up, but I'd gotten rid of most of the contents before hitting the beach. It was why I was only buzzed when Teal found me. Puking in his apartment would probably get me killed.

Now this *is Teal*.

He had a corner unit, huge and clean and no frills, just like Teal. We went through a spotless kitchen to a living room with modular black furniture and an enormous television on the wall.

"What about a second bedroom?" I asked, turning around. "You have two, don't you?"

"Just one. The second room is an office." He pointed to the sofa. "That's yours."

"Shit, you're serious."

"You'll live. You've woken up in strange places before. You can deal with a sofa for one night."

I glared at him. "Why are you always such a bastard to me?"

"Because you're asking for it most of the time," he said, and disappeared down the hall.

By the time he'd returned with blankets, I was so worked up with annoyance I blocked his path. "Maybe you're just an asshole."

"I get paid a lot of money to be an asshole. It's what's kept you out of rehab this long."

I swallowed my scream and closed the gap between us. I couldn't meet his gaze in heels. Barefoot—god only knows what had happened to my shoes—I felt minuscule before him.

"Don't even try to take credit for that, you fucking dick. I'm not completely incapable of making good decisions."

"You make so many bad ones it's hard to tell." He tossed the bedding onto the sofa and stood, hands on hips, scowling back at me. "Anything else you want to say to me?"

"Not a thing," I hissed at him and stepped back.

I couldn't help but smirk at him as I reached down and grasped the hem of my dress. It was over my head in an instant, and there I stood in his perfectly sterile living room wearing nothing but the starfish tattoo on my hip.

Surprise, surprise, he didn't react. His gaze never left my face, and through my anger I started to feel ashamed of myself as I thought about how I must look through his eyes: some over-grown teenager standing bare-assed naked, trying to intimidate a man almost twice her age and twice as mean.

I was ready to cry uncle and turn my back on him when Teal stepped forward. One long stride and we were chest to chest. My stomach fluttered as my cheeks started to burn.

"You know, as I was driving out to the beach to get you I said to myself that one of these days, I'm just going to give that brat what she has coming to her."

His voice was so sinfully low I shivered, and then I realized it wasn't a chill running up my spine, but his fingers. My fingers and toes went numb with disbelief, but the rest of me heated up quickly.

He ran his hands up my arms and left gooseflesh in his wake. Every part of me was so hot with anticipation, and my brain was mush. I couldn't tell whether it was strictly Teal who was doing this to me, or if it was the taboo that was on the verge of being broken.

This can't be a real thing that's happening. Not with Teal.

He reached up beneath my hair and gripped me as he lowered his face. He didn't kiss me. Instead, he rested his cheek against mine and murmured, "Turn around."

For the first time since we'd met, I did exactly what Teal said and when he said it.

I turned, and he pushed me onto my knees on the edge of the sofa. He kept pushing, until my forehead rested against the edge of the seat. He didn't say anything as he pressed his palm against the small of my back.

I had it in my head in an instant: Teal naked and sweating behind me, his large hands clamping down on my hips and his fingers digging in as he pounded into me. The flash was so red hot I moaned and opened up for him.

I moved the way he wanted me to, curving my spine and sticking my ass out.

Teal had other ideas. I heard his movement and bit my bottom lip as I waited for the crinkle of a condom wrapper. Instead, I got cold metal against my lower back, and then the slide of cool leather.

"All the times I hear people say you need rehab or that you're just plain mental, I couldn't get it out of my head that it wasn't the booze at all. Maybe you were looking for something, but couldn't figure out what. No, don't turn around. Stay right where you are."

I closed my eyes. "Please tell me you're not going to do what I think you're going to do."

"Would you try and stop me if I was?"

No, I wouldn't. I was enjoying this too much. I wanted whatever Teal was ready to give me.

He chuckled. "I didn't think so. Your hands, behind your back."

"Is this something you normally do?" I asked, as he looped the belt around my wrists.

"I'm usually on the receiving end."

"Oh."

It was all I could say. I couldn't imagine Teal in my position, feeling what I felt. I was at his mercy, an awareness that was all around me and in my blood.

"I think you need a bit more of a personal touch." He bound me tight and gave me a jerk. "It's about time you found out which one of us is really in charge, don't you think?"

Crack!

First came the sting, and beneath the palm that rested upon me heat spread outward. *Slap. Smack. Love tap.* None of those words came close to describing what happened when his hand connected with my ass.

"How many shots did you say you had tonight?"

It took me a minute to answer. My whole body reeled, not from the slap but from the sheer mind-fuck of being spanked by Teal.

"Uh, I can't remember," I replied, my voice shaking.

"Think about it."

"F-four or five. Probably five."

He ran his hand over my ass, his touch so gentle I quaked. "What else?"

"Two bottles of those vodka coolers. After that, just water or Coke."

"Five shots, two vodka coolers. You called it. Seven."

He brought his hand down again. Before I could catch my breath, he gave me another one.

Teal paused to regain his grip on me, and I could feel his gaze bearing down on me. The way he had me posed left nothing hidden. There was no keeping from him what this was doing to me, or how ready I was for even more. I had never been wetter.

I tugged at my restraints and lifted my ass, a silent invitation.

Teal chuckled and ran his hand along my back. "I'm not going to make it that easy. This is supposed to be, what do they call it? Corrective measures?"

It was my turn to laugh. I rolled my forehead against the sofa edge as jubilation just rolled out of me. "If you don't see a woman ready to be fucked, you must be blind. Your measures aren't working."

"Trust me, they're working."

Four.

Each time he spanked me, the belt tightened.

Five.

The restraints made my hands cold while every other part of me burned up.

Six.

The AC blowing overhead did nothing to cool the sweat across the nape of my neck and back. With my tongue pressed to the roof of my mouth, I breathed hard through my nostrils and waited for the final blow.

Teal pulled on the belt and dragged me upright against his chest. His cock poked through his pants and against my ass as he rubbed his stubbly chin across my shoulder. "I'm going to save the last one for when you really need it."

He dropped his other hand between us and loosened the belt. I made to turn. I wanted to touch him, to feel hot skin beneath my palms, but he looped his arms around my waist and kept me where I was. His breath beat against my neck in shallow puffs.

"Listen to me, and listen close," he said. "Every time you run off and do some scary shit, I wonder what it would feel like if I wasn't around to get you out of it. It's been keeping me up nights lately, and I don't think I can do it for much longer."

The air sucked out of my lungs, and I couldn't draw a breath to replace it. I always figured Teal would be around to catch me whenever I needed him. I didn't think that any of my bullshit took a toll on him.

He pulled me off of the sofa and turned me around. I struggled to work my useless tongue. The disgust that crept up my esophagus was more than guilt, it was loss.

"I don't want you to quit. I don't want you to leave me. I

need you. You know I do. Teal—James, I'll do anything. I'll be anything you want if you stay."

Desperate for his mouth on mine, I slipped my hands to his shoulders.

Cupping my face in his hands, he rested his forehead against mine. "I want you to be you, only...safe."

I held my breath and crashed into chaos as he kissed me.

He did nothing halfway. Neither did I. As he cupped my ass and lifted me off the ground, I dug my nails into his shoulders. I sucked his tongue into my mouth, weightless and dizzy as he carried me through darkness and back into light.

Even when he had set me down on his bed I refused to let go. My hunger for him ruled me. I wrapped my arms around his neck and grasped two fistfuls of hair to keep him there.

He pushed me down with his body, keeping me his willing prisoner as his tongue twisted around mine. Every second that passed my heart drummed against my chest, and I became more feral.

The moment he broke the kiss, I surged up and bit down on his shoulder. Teal cursed and sucked in a deep breath. His growl vibrated against me as I raked my nails down his back.

"That's going to leave a mark," he said as he pushed up off the bed.

"I have your handprint on my ass. Call it even."

I lay back and tried to catch my breath as I watched him undressing for me. It wasn't as though I had never seen Teal stripped down before, and vice versa. He'd been in more hotel rooms with me, stepping aside as I ran, naked, searching for something I'd lost. Teal had been on multiple vacations with me in nothing but a wet swimsuit that left nothing to the imagination when it came to that defined body.

I'd noticed his body, just as I was sure he had noticed mine, but this was different. Watching him unveil inch after inch, I was electric with wanting to run my hands all over him.

The most uncanny thing I'd ever seen was Teal, the silent and stern man who had been by my side all of my adult life, rolling a condom over his hard dick. It gave me a moment's pause, worry tickling at the back of my throat as to whether this was a mistake. I knew I'd never be able to fix it once it was done, and I had been sincere when I told him I didn't want him to leave me.

Teal showed no such hesitation. He knelt on the mattress between my legs and dragged me toward him.

"Don't look like that," he said and watched my face as he positioned the fat tip at the mouth of my pussy. "Just...relax."

His purring tone did it. I melted into the bedding with a sigh.

His gaze remained intense and studying while he filled me up. Buried deep, he lowered himself on top of me, until our faces were barely an inch apart. Flinty eyes gazed into mine.

"I've been wondering lately what you're really like when you come," he muttered as he slowly withdrew. "I've been in the next room enough times to know you're quiet. Or maybe you just haven't gotten off the way you should."

I wrapped my legs around his waist and locked my feet just over his ass. God, if anyone could make me come, it was going to be Teal. His cock twitched as he went deep again. Just having him there, hard and throbbing, was enough to get me halfway there.

"I've spent enough times thinking about all the ways I can make that happen. So many little fantasies cropping up in my head over the years." I gasped as he went over my G-spot, sending a ticklish ripple along my pussy and through my abdomen. Teal let out that low, rumbling laugh. "I'd start by fingering you through your panties in the back of the car during one of your iced-coffee runs."

The pace of his thrusts picked up. He rocked against me, his ass bobbing beneath my heels as he gave me everything and took it away again.

"Maybe bury my face between your thighs while you're waiting to get your makeup done before some appearance," he went on, driving me out of my skull. "Or maybe give the whole world a shock while fucking you from behind on the balcony of some seaside villa. Won't that make a hell of a headline?"

"Five years and you barely say a word, and now this." I pushed down and shuddered as his cock rubbed over the sweet spot again. "Stop talking and fuck me."

He flashed a smile and then rose up over me, glorious and masculine.

With every stroke, the lines between his brows grew a little deeper and his breathing picked up, interspersed with low guttural sounds. His gaze never left my face as he pumped me, and I couldn't look away.

Above me, he was a perfect mixture of the powerful creature I barely knew and this new incarnation intent on the basest needs of his own body.

I wondered how I must appear to him, completely unraveled and moaning and begging for more as he fucked me. Was my transformation as stark as his?

The way he moved was perfection, his hips tilted just right so that every thrust brought a delightful bump against my clit. I tipped my head back with a gasp as the first prelude to an orgasm rippled throughout my pussy.

He pounded me harder. "Just like that. I always knew you'd just let go if I got you in bed."

I would have told him to shut up again, but as he went on

urging me to come I couldn't imagine anything could get me wetter. I reached around and cupped his ass. Muscle went taut beneath my palms each time he pushed deep.

"Oh *fuck*," I managed to push over my tongue as heat flooded me.

I surged up, only to be brought down by Teal's power as he slammed into me. His gaze finally left me as he tipped his head back, his moan cut off with the last thrust that drove me to the center of the bed.

It was as though I had been locked in time, suspended midair by the psychotic pleasure that seemed to have no end. I held on, keeping him deep inside and reveling in the glorious throb that lingered where his dick twitched between my slippery walls.

And then, with a deep breath from each of us, it was over. Teal sagged, his face a mask of exhaustion, and rolled away.

Even as I basked, my body pumping with adrenaline, worry reappeared. We'd burned—*boy*, had we burned—but would Teal go cold on me again?

As though reading my thoughts, he reached out and dragged me into his arms. Tangled up and surrounded by his strength, I felt so safe. I always felt safe with Teal, but with his heart thumping beneath my cheek I felt more than that—I was his to keep safe.

"That was unexpected," he said at last, and laughed when I did. "No, really. I really was going to make you sleep on the sofa."

"It's a good thing you changed tactics. You know how I am in the morning if I haven't had a decent sleep."

I pushed up so I could look at him. Goddamn, if he wasn't smiling. A real fucking ear-to-ear smile.

"I don't want you to quit on me," I said, running my fingers along his bare chest. "You're the only person who doesn't budge when I push. I like that. I like you."

"I think you can convince me to stick around, as long as you don't have me running off after you in the middle of the night again."

"I'd like to think I'll be otherwise occupied in the middle of the night."

I kissed him. I couldn't get enough of him. The phenomenon of his mouth hard and bruising mine, tongue twisting, made me higher than any number of shots could, or stripping down and jumping in the ocean.

And what a high.

"Don't you forget," he muttered, his hand sliding down to my ass, "I still have one more smack left."

"Don't think I won't find a reason to get you to use it." He squeezed my ass and I squealed. It didn't hurt, but I was still a little tender. I settled back down, chin propped on his shoulder, and grinned. "Don't worry, I'll be very good in public, but now that I know what's in store for me you can bet I'll work extra hard at being very bad behind closed doors."

GOING IT ALONE

Lucy Felthouse

As I sat at the table cradling my cup of tea, I contemplated making a run for it. Checking my watch, I ascertained that there were still fifteen more minutes before he was due to arrive, so I could easily leave enough money on the table to pay for my drink and go. I'd be hiding behind my curtains at home before he even arrived.

It wouldn't work, though. He knew where I lived, so if I didn't turn up, he'd come around to my house to see if everything was all right. He was that kind of guy.

I berated myself for thinking about standing him up. He didn't deserve that, not one bit. I was just being a wimp. We'd have a lovely afternoon, I was sure of it. After all, we'd already had dozens of conversations and spent quite a lot of time with each other, and yet this was our first official date. The first time we'd be alone together—albeit in a busy cafe.

The thing that was terrifying me the most wasn't that this was a date, it was that we'd be there without our buffers. Otherwise known as our dogs, Sparky and Chance.

That's how we'd met. I'd been walking Sparky through the park one afternoon and spotted a man and his dog coming in the other direction. I'd expected a polite smile and a nod as we passed, but the canines obviously had other ideas. They'd both strained on their leads to sniff at each other, and as I tugged at Sparky's lead to pull him away, it became apparent that he didn't want to leave. Nor did the other dog. Sighing, I let Sparky do his own thing for a little while, hoping the pair would tire of their bottom-sniffing and allow us all to go our separate ways.

The other dog's owner had obviously had the same idea, and we stood opposite each other as our pets continued their mutual examination. I had the awful thought that Sparky was going to try to mount the other dog and embarrass the hell out of me, so I had to ask, "Is yours a dog or a bitch?"

"A dog."

I heaved a sigh of relief. "Ah, mine too. They certainly seem to like each other."

We looked down, then back up at each other, smiling.

And that was how it started. We ended up chatting about our dogs: their breeds, their age, funny anecdotes about them and so on. The entire time I was thinking about how attractive he was. He had dark cropped hair, lovely hazel eyes and a killer smile. His voice and laugh also had the ability to make the hairs on the back of my neck stand up—in a good way.

By the time we parted ways, dragging our reluctant pets behind us, I had the world's biggest crush. And I didn't even know his name.

Later, it occurred to me to wonder why I hadn't seen him around before. I'd always walked Sparky in that park, and I'd have certainly remembered seeing *him* there.

A few days later, I found out. I was taking a brief pause in my work as a self-employed accountant, and happened to look out of the window just as he walked past with his dog, who I now knew was called Chance.

My brief pause became considerably longer as I scrambled downstairs to put some shoes and a coat on, grab Sparky's lead and head out of the door, with a confused-looking dog padding along behind me. I knew I was behaving like a crazy woman, but I didn't care. Ever since we'd met in the park, I hadn't been able to stop thinking about him. It was insane, and ever so slightly disturbing, but I couldn't help it.

He'd done something to me, and damned if I wasn't going to see it through. It occurred to me that he might not be available or he might not fancy me, but I wasn't bothered. I'd rather know either way, than spend more time torturing myself about it.

I walked toward the park, taking a different route than the one he and Chance had used, meaning we'd probably meet in the middle, like we had before. I just hoped he *was* heading for the park. There were plenty of other places he could have gone, and I couldn't wander aimlessly around the entire village looking for him. That would be full-on stalker behavior, as opposed to the milder form I was adopting now.

Thankfully, though, my scheming paid off. As planned, we met in the middle of the park. As soon as we got close, our respective animals' joy at seeing each other meant it would be almost impossible to pass by without talking again.

"Hello again," he said, as we stood side by side, watching our excitable pets.

"Hi," I replied, biting back the next words that wanted to come out of my mouth. *Fancy seeing you here.*

"Shall we let 'em off for a run?" he said, indicating the dogs.

My response was to bend and unclip Sparky's lead from his

collar. My new crush did the same for Chance. They immediately bounded off, playing some crazy game of chase, and I headed toward a nearby bench with the guy in tow.

This time, I found out more about him. His name was Jake, and he'd just moved to the area. That explained why I hadn't seen him before. From there, we chatted about a variety of things, and although I didn't ask him outright, the way he spoke led me to believe he was free and single. I mentally rejoiced. Our talk remained fairly superficial, and any lull in conversation was taken up by the antics of the dogs, who occasionally bounded over to us to say hello in their panting doggy way, leaving muddy paw prints on our clothes, then running off again.

Which is why I was so terrified of our being on an actual date. Up until now, the dogs had always been there as a talking point if we ran out of things to say, and an excuse to go home after an appropriate length of time. They'd helped us avoid awkward silences and given us an excuse to be there in the first place.

This time, however, we were going it alone. I felt pressured to be witty and entertaining and make sparkling conversation. The fact that I really liked him made it so much worse. I was just about to make a mental list of things we could talk about when he walked in. I had a few seconds to admire him before he glanced in my direction and smiled before heading over to the table.

Desperate not to show my nervousness, I went for the nonchalant look, taking a sip of my tea and hoping that he didn't notice when I dribbled some down my chin. I swept the back of my hand across my face as subtly as possible and was once again cradling my cup when Jake reached me.

"Hi, Debbie," he said, his proximity already causing my heart rate to increase, "can I get you a top up?" He indicated my drink.

"Yes, please. That would be lovely. Tea with milk and two sugars, please."

Giving a nod, Jake made his way to the counter. I watched him go, enjoying the spectacular view of his rear end, and desperately hoping he wouldn't turn and catch me looking.

Soon, he was back with our drinks and he quickly engaged me in conversation. We'd already covered all the basic stuff people talk about in our many chats in the park, so we were onto deeper stuff, like exes, education, family; that kind of thing. It wasn't until I finished my second drink—which was tepid by then—that I happened to glance at my watch.

"Bloody hell, is that the time?" I blurted out before I could stop myself.

Jake raised an eyebrow. "You got somewhere else you need to be?"

"No, not at all. I just didn't realize we'd been here that long. I bet poor Sparky's crossing his legs though!"

Jake grinned. "I bet he is. I left Chance in the garden, so he'll be fine. Do you need to go back and check on him? I'll walk you back if you want."

I don't know what it was that made me suddenly so bold, but my next words surprised even me. "I've got a better idea." I lowered my voice. "Rather than paying for more tea here, why don't we go back to my house and have some for free? Or you can even have something else to drink, if you like!"

"Oooh, you do spoil me," Jake said with a wink, sipping the last of his drink. "But I like your idea very much. Just let me go and settle our bill and I'll meet you outside."

Before I could mention paying my share, he'd jumped up and was already moving to the counter. Sighing happily, I made sure everything was in my bag, grabbed my coat and headed outside. I was just thinking about how hot Jake was and wondering if he fancied me as much as I fancied him when he appeared next to me.

"Ready?"

"Yep. Sure you can handle the long walk?" I was being sarcastic, of course. My house was just a few minutes' walk away.

"Oh, I think so. There's life in the old boy, yet!"

I elbowed him playfully in the side. "Hey, if you're an old boy, then that makes me an old girl!"

"How so?"

"Well, I'm only a year younger than you."

We had a tongue-in-cheek argument about who was old and who wasn't, and soon we were back at my house. Once I'd grabbed my keys and unlocked the back door, we were met by an excitable Sparky, who bounded around our legs a couple of times, then disappeared into the garden. We shrugged off our coats and hung them on the rack by the door, which I left open so Sparky could get back in. Then I moved into the kitchen and filled and flicked on the kettle.

I turned to ask Jake what he wanted to drink, fully expecting him to be looking around the house—I know I would have been had the roles been reversed—but instead was startled to find him standing close behind me.

"Oh, h-hello," I said, his proximity making me nervous, "you all right?"

"Yes," he replied quietly. His intense gaze made my heart pound, and an unexpected rush of arousal headed to my groin. He said nothing else, just continued to look at me, and I had to resist the temptation to squirm.

"Are you all right"—he took a step closer, trapping me between his warm body and the work top—"with this?"

I gulped. "Y-yes."

"Good, because I'd really like to kiss you now."

My mouth went dry, and I couldn't speak. Instead, I nodded.

Jake took that as his cue—thankfully—and leaned toward me. I closed my eyes, and felt goose bumps wash over my body in anticipation of his lips touching mine. In reality, the wait was only milliseconds, but it felt like longer. Perhaps because I'd been daydreaming about it for so damn long.

Finally, his mouth pressed against mine. His kiss was chaste at first, but the longer our lips were in contact, the more I wanted. By the time I felt Jake's tongue seeking entry to my mouth, I was hungry for it. Wrapping my arms around his neck, I pulled him more tightly to me. A little thrill of pleasure ran through me as I felt his erection pressing against my stomach.

Before things could get too hot and heavy in the kitchen, however, we were interrupted by Sparky jumping up at us, no doubt wondering what he was missing out on. Jake and I parted, laughing at the dog's antics, though I silently cursed him. Things had been going so well.

"Do you, uh, want to take this upstairs?" Jake said, his face serious again now.

I nodded emphatically, then took his hand and led him up to my bedroom. I didn't trust myself to speak, so I hoped that my body language would do all the talking.

Closing the door behind us, I prayed my nerve wouldn't give out on me now. We'd gotten this far, so he obviously wanted to be with me, and hopefully as more than just a one-off.

I walked over to where Jake stood beside my bed—I'm an obsessively tidy person, so I didn't have to worry about embarrassing things being strewn about my room—and put my hands on the hem of his T-shirt. He grinned down at me, which bolstered my confidence, and I pushed the material up his torso, revealing a very attractive body. He wasn't a bodybuilder, not by any stretch of the imagination, but he clearly looked after himself. A scattering of dark hair grew over his pecs and tapered down his stomach, before disappearing into the waistband of his jeans.

A moan escaped my lips, and I blushed as Jake laughed. "Well, it's nice to be appreciated. Care to return the favor?"

He tugged the top over his head and dropped it on the floor. Then he kicked off his shoes. I followed suit, removing my boots, but was more hesitant when it came to my blouse. Jake wasn't so reticent. He grabbed my hands and pulled me to him.

"Debbie, you're beautiful," he said, tucking my hair behind my ears, "so let me see you."

My face colored again, but I undid the buttons of my shirt and removed it. A low whistle came from Jake.

"Honey, tell me you have condoms, because I want you bad."

His blatant and oh-so-sexy words finally pushed me through the barrier of shyness, and my arousal took over. Grinning at him, I began to remove the rest of my clothes, hoping he would continue. He did, and soon we were both totally naked.

With a sauciness that I didn't know I had in me, I shoved Jake so he fell backward onto my bed, then grabbed a condom from my bedside drawer—luckily it was still in date—and handed it to him. Joining him on the bed, I watched as he undid the rubber and rolled it down his erect cock. My pussy was so swollen by now that it felt heavy, and I was desperate to have Jake's thick dick inside it, fucking me.

My rational, shy mind having fled, I said the words out loud, then clapped a hand over my mouth in shock.

Raising an eyebrow, Jake said, "Why is your hand over your mouth? Do you want to fuck me, or not?"

"Of course," I whispered, "I'm just not normally this forward."

Jake shifted up the bed so his head was on the pillows, and held out a hand.

"I think we're beyond all that now, don't you? I want you, you want me. Now come here."

I did as he said, making to lie beside him, but he stopped me.

"No, not there. On top of me. I said I wanted you *bad*, remember? And that means now. We've got plenty of time to go slow, later. Or tomorrow. Or the day after."

Well, he'd certainly answered my question about it being a one-off. Glad we were on the same page, I straddled him, kneeling so my pussy was hovering just over his cock. I looked at his face, and the expression on it sent another jolt of lust to my already overloaded cunt. He was rapt, watching me, waiting for me to sink my pussy onto his eager cock.

"Debbie," he said, his voice almost a whisper, "please..."

I grasped his latex-covered shaft and lifted it so the tip of his prick was in the right position. Then, unable to wait any longer, I dropped down onto him. Our mutual groans filled the room, and I collapsed down onto his chest, wanting to have as much contact as possible.

I captured his bottom lip with my teeth, giving a playful nip. I was surprised to feel his cock twitch inside me.

"Oh," I said, releasing him with a grin, "so you're into a bit of pain, are you?"

"I'm into a lot of things, Debbie, and I'm sure you are, too. But we've got plenty of time for all that. Now please, just fuck me."

I was happy to oblige. I rolled my hips, savoring the feel of his cock stretching me, and the way my clit rubbed against his body. I increased my pace, closing my eyes as waves of pleasure rolled over and over me, and I felt my orgasm growing close, just waiting to be triggered.

Then, just as I was really getting into a rhythm, Jake's hands gripped my hips and he rolled us over so he was on top.

"I'm really sorry, babe, but you're driving me crazy. In a good way." His smile was bright, almost manic with his lust. "And I really have to come. Hold on tight."

Crossing my ankles around his legs and my arms around his neck, I did as I was bidden. And boy, was I glad I did. After a couple of thrusts, Jake began to fuck me like a man possessed. I clung on to him, rendered silent by extreme pleasure. Then, as I felt my cunt tighten around him, I planted my feet on the bed, meeting him thrust for thrust until my climax hit with a delicious vengeance and I stuffed a corner of a pillow into my mouth to stifle my screams.

Jake clearly couldn't hold out as my pussy contracted around him, and he gave a series of shallow thrusts before letting out a roar and freezing in place. His cock leapt and twitched, releasing its load inside the rubber.

Jake leaned down to me, propping his weight on his forearms, and gave me a toe-curling kiss that was hot enough to get me started all over again.

"Fucking hell," he said, pulling away, "that was so hot. I feel like I was waiting forever to do that."

"Me too," I replied. "I fancied you almost as soon as we met."

"Really? I must confess, the feeling was mutual."

"So why did it take you so long to ask me out?"

"Why didn't you ask *me* out?"

My response was to reach up and tickle his ribs. He rolled off me with a guffaw. Discarding the condom, he reached over to retaliate for my tickle, and as we fell about the bed in a series of squeals and giggles, I realized it didn't matter who had asked who out.

All that mattered was now and what happened next. And as I noticed his cock begin to stiffen again, I suspected what happened next was going to be very nice indeed.

CLOSING THE DEAL

Kelly Maher

The salt-tinged breeze blew tendrils of hair across her face. Julia dragged them back behind the earpiece of her sunglasses. Sand squished between her toes with every step. The blue sea to her right called a siren song to her, but she wasn't ready for her worries to be washed away. Her navy-blue suit wouldn't survive a dunking in salt water either.

She'd hoped the extra days on St. Thomas would have cleared the mental brush, letting her see a solution to how to handle Paul. Her shoulders slumped as marimba trilled from her pocket. Her last morning walk to herself was over. Brunch awaited inside the conference center, and she needed to stop in her villa to finish dressing. She hurried back across the sand, enjoying the feel of her leg muscles working against the drag. Wood scoured soft by years of weathering met her feet when she hit the porch. She'd heard her neighbor come in late last night but had yet to catch sight of who it might be.

The cool shade of her villa and the terrazzo tile blunted the edge of the tropical heat as the sun started its midday arc. In her bedroom, she pulled a pair of thigh-highs from a drawer. She might be here for work, but she couldn't bring herself to wear full tights in this climate. Especially as she still needed to walk to the conference center. Luckily, a brick walkway led from the back door of her villa to the central resort area, so she could manage heels. She grabbed her satchel and headed out the door.

She'd made it only a couple of hundred feet down the path when she heard a bang behind her. She looked over her shoulder and saw it was her neighbor. Dark suit, short copper hair, a good half-foot taller than her even in the heels. Her eyes widened.

Paul.

She turned back around and ran for the resort, not caring that her heels echoed with every step. The conference center loomed out of the vegetation as she rounded the corner. Through the glass walls she could see her boss and their vice president standing near the door. She paused to catch her breath. She was a professional. Inner turmoil had no place in international business.

Closing her eyes, she pictured the centering image her yoga instructor had taught her. Five seconds and she had herself in hand, her decidedly non-work-colleague feelings for Paul shoved into a tiny mental box.

The door opened as she approached and arctic air spilled out, cooling her down even further.

"Julia, there you are! Did you have a nice little vacation?" Her vice president was one of those guys who had gotten to his level due to a good dose of charm. At least he was one of the few who were as willing to dole out credit as take it for themselves.

"Yes, sir. Thank you. I've got all of the figures for the Monteblanca side of the deal ready."

"Wonderful. Go on in and grab some grub. We're still waiting on a few players."

She nodded to her boss and did as directed. A tropical bounty was laid out on the side table. She picked at some fruit and eggs for protein. She glanced through the windows on the conference room door and saw Paul had arrived and been cornered by her boss. Taking advantage of his delay, she moved to the corner where another coworker already sat. As he was her counterpart for another section of this hydra of a deal, they compared notes as they ate.

Paul walked into the room. Even though she tried to keep her body under control so as not to draw his attention, her breath hitched. He was with her boss, so instead of making a beeline for her, he was herded to the buffet.

However, she'd underestimated him, as he quickly filled his plate and distracted her boss by snagging another coworker before heading her way. There were no other unoccupied chairs in their corner, which was why she selected it. He made room anyway.

"Hey, Dave. Do you mind if I sit next to Julia? There are some last-minute projections I want to go over with her before we start."

"Sure, man. Hey, want to hit the driving range when we're done here?"

She bored a hole into the opposite wall with her gaze as she fought the compulsion to look at him.

"Maybe. I got in late last night and the jet lag's still killing me. I may go for a swim in the ocean. Got to take advantage of being put up in a beachside villa."

"Definitely. Catch you later. See you, Julia."

"Later, Dave." She waited until Paul sat and she saw no one paying them much attention. "Did you have to sit there?"

He speared a piece of pineapple. Chewed it. "We need to talk."

"Not here."

"I do have some projections for you."

She snuck a glare at him before turning her attention back to her own food. "You could have emailed it to me."

"You were walking on the beach when I got them. I did forward the info to you, but considering when you got back, I don't think you've checked it yet."

"You were watching me?"

"Hey, I didn't realize you were my neighbor until this morning. I happened to catch you heading out when I was drinking my morning coffee."

"You're impossible."

"You were the one who ran out. Two days later I heard through the grapevine you'd flown down here early. And it was only thanks to your secretary that I knew you'd gotten home safe that night. You could have at least texted me."

"We were done."

The weight of his gaze pressed on her until she met it. "Not with everything."

She glanced around the room. The vice president had come in with who she assumed were the members of the other company he'd been waiting on. She turned back to Paul and lowered her brows. "Yes, everything. We're work colleagues. That is it. End of story."

Paul opened his mouth to reply, but the meeting was called to order. He never had a chance to bring the topic up for the rest of the morning. They worked through lunch, a catered affair as lavish as the brunch. At one point in the afternoon when the bulk of her work had been presented and assessed, she excused herself to use the restroom.

She finished her business and enjoyed the luxury setting with a touch-up of lotion and reset her hairstyle. Opening the door, she found Paul standing there.

"What—?"

He pushed in, and closed and locked the door behind him.

"What are you doing? Let me out."

"I will. Someone was coming down the hall behind me and I don't want us caught." As if on cue, the handle jerked up and down.

She narrowed her eyes and hissed at him. "You planned that."

He held up his hand with thumb and pinkie folded in and the other three fingers standing. "Scout's honor, I didn't. I hadn't realized you were even in this bathroom until I opened the door."

"This is the one closest to the conference room."

"Even more reason not to get caught with the bosses around."

She opened her mouth, but nothing would come out. She waved her hand in front of her face as if to push him out of her mind and reached for the door.

His hand, calloused on the edges and warm, closed around her wrist. "Give it a moment in case anyone else happens to be out there and saw me come in."

"I need to get back there."

"Your part's done for the day. You've got time."

She closed her eyes to block out the warm gray of his. Darts of lust radiated from where he touched her. She could not give in. So what if he thought her a runner? That was a hell of a lot better than compromising their work relationship for a one-night stand.

His thumb rubbed her inner wrist. She licked her lips.

"Come on, Jules. Give me a shot here."

Her eyes flashed open as she felt his hot breath on the skin behind her ear. "Paul."

"You leaving me hurt. And I don't mean physically. I thought I meant more to you."

"We work together."

He licked the hollow and nipped her earlobe. "We're both adults. Neither of us is the boss. Unless you want to role-play. Then I'm all over that. You can call me in to your office and reprimand me all you want."

Her nipples hardened and her breath shuddered out. A corner of her mind was screaming to turn him down and get the hell out of there. Run far and fast. She'd done that last time. But here he was.

The fingers of his free hand ran the length of her skirt. With each pass, he edged the hem up a little bit more. "I've been wanting you for ages, Jules. It was all I could do to keep my hands off of you until the end of this project."

Her fingers flexed into the soft flannel of his suit. Hard muscle resisted the pressure. She bit her lip. They could do this. *What happens in St. Thomas stays in St. Thomas, right?*

"Jules?" His fingers skated up the inner face of her leg. Found the edge of her thigh high and traced it. Heat sizzled in her blood.

"On one condition."

He kissed along her jawline until their eyes met. "What?"

His fingers moved closer to where the silk of her panties provided a faint barrier. Her head fell back as she reached for that final contact.

"Jules. What's your condition?"

"Only here. This can only happen here."

His fingers paused an inch from where she was desperate to feel them. "What if I don't accept?"

The words sliced through the fog of lust wreathing her brain. "You have to."

He shook his head, but his hands remained where they were. "I want you. I really, really want you. I want you beyond work, beyond here."

She should be backing away, but her body refused to break from his touch. "I can only give you here and now."

His fingers pressed in. "You can give me so much more, Jules, and I can do the same. Give us a chance."

He didn't demand. Her life would be easier if he did. Then she could have dismissed him like she had the last coworker who thought long nights together in the office required *payback*. "I can't decide now."

Fingertips circled in place, warming her where they touched. "How about this? We've got three days here. Let me use those three days to convince you to give us a shot beyond here."

She drew in a deep breath. It was reasonable. Even though his hands were almost in her panties, her brains hadn't completely shorted and she knew this was an even compromise. She met his gaze. "Fine. Three days."

The white of his teeth gleamed as he grinned. "I'm not going to let you regret it." With that, he leaned in and kissed her.

Firm lips massaged hers. Her tongue darted out to taste him. A hint of pineapple and coffee. She moaned as his fingers finally breached the silk. He nipped her lip. "Quiet. Someone may be out there."

Two long digits eased into her sheath, and she blocked out everything but riding them.

"That's it. Fuck my fingers." His thumb joined in and played with her clit.

Her orgasm streaked through her and she clenched down on him.

"Fuck."

She could feel a faint tremble where she touched him. Her lungs panted in and out as the aftershocks hit. Her muscles protested as he pulled out. She wanted his cock, but her inner alarm was ringing that their time had run out.

He eased her against the wall and went to the sink where he washed his hands and reached for a hand towel and wetted it. He handed it to her. A bit embarrassed, she turned to the corner, lifted her skirt and washed as best she could.

When she turned around, he was there. He kissed her again, and she melted against him. She felt him smile against her lips before he broke away. "Later. I'll go first. Lock the door behind me and give it a couple of minutes before coming back."

She nodded and followed the plan after applying cold compresses to every pulse point she could reach. When she returned, it was in the middle of a heavy round of negotiations so no one paid attention to her. Once back in her seat, she clenched her thighs together and tried not to focus on Paul sitting next to her. She managed to get through the rest of the meeting without anyone commenting on her prolonged absence.

When they left for the night, Paul was cornered by one of the other acquisitions teams, so she took the opportunity to hurry back to the villa.

As soon as she locked the door behind her, she dithered. A crossroad stood before her, and she didn't know which way to turn. One direction and she could continue on as she had been with a partnership in her reach. The other, a relationship with a man who deserved a woman committed to making it work. She wasn't sure she had it in her to devote the time needed to cultivate that kind of connection.

She didn't know how long Paul would be delayed, so if she were going to do something, it had to be now. The open door to her bedroom called to her, but where would she go? It wasn't like she could race back to New York. Exchanging the villa for a room in the main resort was downright cowardly.

She had to be honest with herself. Paul had given her one of her top five orgasms. She wanted more. Which meant she needed to truly agree to his terms of giving him a chance. What was she really afraid of?

Paul? No. She knew if things didn't work out, he'd chalk it up as an experience learned.

Herself? Possibly. Her track record in picking guys wasn't the best. Wasn't the worst either. None of her exes had ever hit or disparaged her, but neither had they done anything to live life beyond their college glory years. Paul's ambition had been one of the initial attractors for her. He wanted more and worked hard to get it.

Maybe that was it. What if Paul wanted more than she could give? *Damn, I am seriously overthinking this.* Disgusted with her waffling, she made her decision. *Like Dad always said, putting an application in doesn't mean you have to take the damn job.*

She went into her bedroom and stripped out of her suit and underwear. The faint musk that filled the room when she removed her panties set her blood to a low level simmer as she remembered the feel of Paul's fingers working her.

A knock on her door shocked her back into reality. Pulling on her robe, she hoped it was Paul. If not, she was going to plead a case of disagreeable food.

She checked the peephole and Paul stood on the other side, the lines of his suit wilting in the early evening heat. Opening the door enough to stick her head out, she looked him over. "Yes?"

His smile was easy. "How about I call room service for

dinner and meet you back here in fifteen minutes?"

"It's a little early for dinner."

"But I can come over in fifteen minutes?"

She took a deep breath. "Sure."

His smile widened to a grin. "Great."

She closed the door and leaned back against it. One step at a time. She debated changing, but couldn't think of what to wear and didn't want to waste time figuring it out. In the kitchenette, she pulled out a couple of short glasses. Her first day here, she'd bought a bottle of rum but hadn't opened it.

This time the knock came from the beachside entrance. The glass door hid nothing from view. Something to remember even though people rarely wandered down this way as they were at the end of the line of villas and the beach was private property. Paul was dressed in shorts and a loose Tommy Bahama shirt. His skin had the paleness of a man who spent more time in the office than in the sun, but he had a bit of color. Probably from running. She'd once overheard him say he liked to run through Central Park at least twice a week. Light-brown hair sprinkled his arms and legs, complementing the light copper of his head and brows.

He raised his fist again and knocked while he smiled at her. She jerked out of her stasis and opened the door.

"You okay?"

She nodded. "I think so."

He frowned. "That doesn't sound promising. Do you want me to leave?"

"Nope. I was pouring drinks in the kitchen. Do you like rum?"

His shoulders relaxed. She hadn't realized how tense he must have been. "Sure. I'll try anything once. What brand?"

"I'm not sure. I picked it up in the city market my first day here." She grabbed the glasses and looked at the label. Laughed. "All it says is *St. Thomas Finest*. I guess we're living danger-ously."

"I guess we are."

She shivered as she felt the words whisper across the back of her neck. He reached around her and took the glasses and bottle without touching her. She followed him back into the sitting area. Instead of taking advantage of the love seat, he sat down in one of the club chairs. The move surprised her.

"You're being awfully circumspect." She pulled the other club chair closer and folded her legs beneath her as she sat, pulling the hem of her robe over her knees.

"When a woman you're interested in runs off in the middle of what you thought was the beginning of an exceptional night and she gives you a second chance, you don't want to repeat the past." He poured two fingers of rum into each glass and handed one to her.

She sipped and let the mellow liquor spread its warmth through her. "Most guys would say 'fuck it' and forget about her."

He met her gaze straight on. "I'm not most guys."

She let the silence spin out between them and then set her glass back down on the table. "No, you're not."

"Tell me why, Jules. I deserve that."

He did. The urge to reach for the glass of liquor once again tempted, but she left the glass on the table. "I don't know if I have it in me to give a relationship, any romantic relationship, the time it deserves. I can taste a partnership. To get it, I have to work sixty or more hours a week." She leaned forward and rested her elbows on her knees. "I love that, Paul. I love helping to put together complex deals. Even worse, if I got involved with a coworker, people might think I was only biding my time before bagging someone for marriage." She broke off eye contact and looked out the wall of windows to the ocean. "Everything I've worked for will be for nothing."

"I get it."

She turned back to him. Gave him a sad smile. "Really? I don't think a lot of guys, especially white guys, get what it's like to constantly need to prove yourself in the workplace."

He raised his glass in acknowledgment. "We never talked about our families. My mom raised me, my sister and my brother by herself. Dad died from cancer in his thirties. He left some life insurance but it wasn't much. Mom worked her way up from office secretary to one of the top salespeople in her company. She got a lot of shit from her coworkers, and I'm sure my siblings and I don't know the half of it. I respect what you're doing, Jules. I only want the opportunity to get to know you better, and, hopefully, have you get to know me better."

She stood and held her hand out to him.

His brows arched down into a *V*. He tilted his head up to meet her eyes. "What?"

The heat bloomed within her and she let it shine in her smile. "Come with me."

His glass hit the edge of the table, and a few drops of rum spilled out. They both laughed, his tinged with self-deprecating humor and hers with the power he'd handed to her.

He twined his fingers with hers. Just before she opened the door to her bedroom, he tugged on them. She turned back and arched a brow.

Leaning down, he brushed a kiss against her lips before resting his forehead on hers. "Don't kick my ego in the balls, okay? There's only so much I can take."

She kissed him, teasing him with her tongue. After a minute she pulled back. "I promise. No ego kicking. I do want this."

"And after?"

"We'll sort it out as it happens. That's all I can give you."

The gray of his eyes softened as he peered into her soul. "Thank you."

He gripped the handle of her door and opened it. He bent and swept her up into his arms. She shrieked at the sudden change in balance. Paul wasn't a scrawny man, but neither was she a lightweight herself. He juggled her until she wrapped her arms around his shoulders.

Early evening light streamed in through the windows ringing the top third of the walls of the bedroom. He placed her down on the bed and followed her down, blanketing her with his body. She spread her legs to cradle his hips. The feel of him full against her satisfied something she hadn't realized her soul had been craving.

Strong lips commanded hers. She remembered the feel of them from their one aborted night together and reveled in the changes in pressure she liked best. Eventually, he teased her lips open with his tongue and they dueled for supremacy.

His hand worked the robe's tie at her waist until it slithered open. They both moaned when he cupped her breast. Her nipples hardened even further as he massaged the swelling mound.

She ground her hips against his, working the erection lining the placket. He broke the kiss and laid his head against her neck as he heaved in a breath.

"Damn, woman." He pushed up and kneeled between her thighs.

She slipped her arms from the robe and sat up. Helped him with removing his shirt. A few buttons popped off. He reached for his fly, but she stayed his hands. His ridged abdomen flexed in front of her as he sucked in air. She outlined each muscle with kisses.

At the waistband of his shorts, she nipped the skin at the top of the fly. He wound his fingers through her hair as she licked the hurt. She undid the buttons and pushed down his shorts and briefs. His cock begged for attention. The hair surrounding its base was a bit darker than the hair on his head. She strung kisses along its length and watched as the vessels beneath the skin pulsed even harder.

Taking the tip into her mouth, she delicately sucked as she squeezed the root. He groaned and pulled away. "God, Jules. I need to last here."

She laughed as he pushed her back onto the pillows. He stepped off the bed and shed his shorts. From the back pocket of them, he pulled out a foil packet and tossed it on to the bed. Appreciating his preparedness, she held it up. "Want me to put it on?"

He grinned. "No. You'll have me shooting off before you get it half on. This is all I brought with me, so it's got to last."

"No night of debauchery planned?"

He climbed back onto the bed and settled himself next to her. Running a hand down from her neck to her hip, he smiled. "Definitely hoped for, but nope, no planning."

Bending his neck, he dropped a kiss on her shoulder. She curled up to wrap herself around him, but he pushed down on the other shoulder, pinning her to the bed. He worshipped her body. Kisses, bites, licks. He paid homage to every inch of her. At the apex of her thighs, he buried his face into her curls and licked her out until she gave a short scream. The orgasm was only a prelude as he surged back up.

He grabbed the packet and ripped it open, sliding the latex down his shaft. He hooked one arm under one of her thighs and positioned himself with his other hand. Speared into her. She shuddered. The first thrust of a cock was one of her favorite parts of sex. The mini-orgasm had taken the edge off, but as he worked her—short thrusts, mixed with the odd long thrust and pause—the heat became incendiary. She clutched at his arms but couldn't find purchase.

The palm of the hand not holding her leg up pressed down on her mons, rubbing her clit with every movement of his hips. The pressure ensured she felt every ridge of his cock. She clamped down on him and his control finally broke. He pounded into her. Her orgasm washed over her and she screamed. He jerked and groaned above her, then collapsed on top of her.

Neither moved for an eternity. Finally, he slipped out of her and got off the bed to dispose of the used condom. He left the room for a few minutes and came back with a wet washcloth. Cleaned her as he murmured sweet nothings in her ear. She smiled and petted the back of his neck. He left once more and then came back in and crawled into bed with her. Pulled the sheets around them and her into his arms. Kissed her temple.

"How about it? Room service and then a night of debauchery?"

She somehow found it in herself to laugh. "Sure. That sounds wonderful." She kissed him to seal the deal.

WHATEVER IT TAKES

Kristina Wright

"The twins have baseball practice at five o'clock. Can you get Meredith to her dance class?" I ask, holding the phone between my ear and shoulder as I navigate the Jeep through the purgatory known as the after-school pick-up line. "I'll take Luke and Joey to baseball and pick up Trevor at Reya's house when they're done with their project. And if you can get Meredith to and from dance and pick up Chinese on the way home, we can eat dinner around seven."

"I can drop her off and pick her up, but I need to get downtown before six and pick up the hardware for the cabinets in the garage so I can get those installed this weekend," David says. "She'll be okay at dance class alone, right?"

I bite my lip. "Probably. Yeah, she'll be fine. Just ask Savannah's mother to keep an eye on her until you get back. Class is over at six-thirty, so don't get stuck in traffic."

"I'll do my best, honey. Now, which one is Savannah's mother?"

"Can't remember her name," I say, waving out the car

window to five-year-old twins, Luke and Joey. They amble over to the car, dragging their backpacks along the sidewalk, and climb inside. "She's the one with the—um—large assets."

Luke giggles and Joey hollers from the backseat, "That means she has big boobs!"

Damn public school. My babies are learning things I certainly wasn't teaching them or ready for them to learn.

David laughs. "Got it. I definitely remember her. Be careful, babe. I'll see you at home. Eventually."

I feel a pang of jealousy as I hang up. Not over Savannah's mother; well, not entirely. But a surge of emptiness that has nothing to do with David being attracted to other women and everything to do with the fact that we hardly see each other. Four kids, one dog, three cats, a hamster, a guinea pig, a mortgage we can barely afford—and two exhausted parents and partners, trying to hold it all together.

I'm blinking back tears and finally pulling out of the school's parking lot when my phone rings. Blindly, I reach for it on the passenger seat. "Yeah?"

"I'm going to fuck you tonight, you know. Long and slow and hard and deep."

Heat suffuses my cheeks, still damp from my tears. "Are you now?"

"Yeah, baby. I miss you. I can't wait to be inside you."

And just like that, he's gone.

"Was that Daddy?" Luke asks.

"Uh, no," I mutter, pressing my thighs together as I drive. "That was *David*."

I hear the boys giggle at Mommy's silly joke, but it's no joke. He may be Daddy to them, but he has a way of reminding me of just who he is to me. *David*. Mine. And I can't wait to see that guy.

* * *

By the time we get all the kids home, fed, bathed, homework checked, stories read, songs sung and last round of video games played, I think he's forgotten all about his wicked promise. I haven't, but there are still dishes to do and a load of laundry to haul upstairs. I can hear David puttering in the garage sorting the recycle bin to go out to the curb as I walk past the door to the laundry room and my anticipation quickly turns to annoyance.

I stomp up the stairs, dropping panties and socks as I go and bending to retrieve them, when I hear his voice and feel the slap of his hand on my bottom.

"Nice ass, baby. I can't wait to see it naked."

And—boom—just like that, I'm right back in the car, with his voice in my ear and my panties dampening. I can't see him under the cascade of my hair as I'm bent over on the stairs, precariously balancing a laundry basket on my hip, but I can hear the inflection in his soft-spoken voice. His tone isn't playful; it's serious as a heart attack.

When he says, "Give me that laundry basket and get your cute ass to bed," I don't argue. I hand him the basket and high-tail it down the hall, turning a mother's ear to each of the closed doors along the way. All is quiet and peaceful. For now.

He follows me and closes the bedroom door behind him, locking it. The laundry basket is tossed in the corner, clothes tumbling out, but I don't care and I can tell by the way he's not even noticing the mess that he'll be happy to live out of the basket if it means we get down to the business.

The clothes come off quickly, silently. I'd say we have this thing down to a science, but "science" suggests there's no emotion, no passion, it's just another chore to accomplish. And, oh my, it isn't that at all. It's heat and fire and the way he's watching me strip off my capris while I'm studying the hair on his forearms as he unbuttons the top couple of buttons of his shirt before he gets impatient and pulls it over his head like one of the kids would. But I'm not thinking about the kids. Or the laundry. Or the dog who is whining at the door because she hates to be locked out of our room. I'm only thinking about him—this man of mine— and how it's going to feel when he presses me into the mattress, pinned at my hands and my hips by his fingers entwined with mine and his cock buried inside me.

We're naked in under a minute, but it's too long. I need him. He needs me. We tumble down to the bed sideways and I hook my leg around his hip and draw him closer. He's hard, of course, his erection freed from the confines of his jeans and underwear now and nudging my belly. I'm wet and hot already, no foreplay needed, but that doesn't stop him.

"Damn, baby, I've been thinking about this all day," he mutters, licking along the rim of my ear before pressing his lips to my neck. "I've missed you so much."

"Did Savannah's mother get you all riled up?"

He pulls back to look at me, see if I'm serious or just playing. Our fantasies go in all different kinds of directions sometimes, even to other partners. But I get so little of David these days, I'm not in the mood to play that game. I have no desire to share. I want him all to myself right now.

"You're not serious?" he asks, determining from my expression that I'm not looking for a fantasy.

I shake my head, not trusting my voice but needing to say something. "No, not really. You don't have any more time than I do for—"

"It's not about time," he says, his voice rough. "You're it, babe. You know that. Just you and me—" He gestures toward the closed door. "And the rest of our tribe. That's all I want. All I've ever wanted."

As if to make his point, he pushes against me, his rigid cock a warm, insistent reminder that he does, in fact, want me. Right *now.*

I laugh. I can't help it. It's probably louder than it should be, given the sleeping children just down the hall, but sometimes I need to hear him say what he is saying now. Remind me of what I already know.

"Yeah, I know," I mutter, my cheeks flushing from embarrassment rather than desire. "I just miss the alone time with you. It's just been—"

"Crazy lately," he finishes for me, twirling my nipple between his fingers. "Yeah, I know. We need to work on that. Farm the kids out to their friends and spend some quality time together making up for lost time."

He tweaks the other nipple for good measure and I can feel myself slipping into a head space that will make rational conversation impossible. But still, I have to add, "It's not just me, right? You feel the same way?"

His mouth follows the path of his fingers, sucking and nibbling my nipples until they are aching and hard. "What do you think?" he mumbles, his mouth full of my flesh.

"I think you'd better do something with that hard-on before I lose what's left of my mind."

He drags my leg higher up on his hip, the broad tip of his cock nudging my wetness. "Oh really? And what happens when you lose your mind?"

I use my weight as leverage to roll him over on his back, his erection slipping into me as if that's where it is meant to be. And it is. This is home. His and mine. We're home. I seat myself more firmly and rock back.

"I take over," I say, breathless with the anticipation of pleasure. "And you are helpless to do my bidding."

It's his turn to laugh, a full-bellied laugh that causes his cock to jerk inside me and make me catch my breath. A hint of things to come, so to speak, even while we're still caught between the realities of life and our own intense need for each other. I clench my thighs around his hips and grind on his cock, enjoying every sensation.

His laughter stops suddenly and he's pulling me down to him, kissing me softly even as he thrusts up into me. I gasp into his open mouth and he thrusts again, hitting that sweet spot he knows so well.

"No fair," I mumble against his lips. "You're playing dirty."

He licks my bottom lip, then sinks his teeth into it just hard enough to make every nerve tingle. "You like it dirty."

He's right, of course. I may be on top, but there's no doubt who is controlling things at the moment, and I love it that way. His teeth tugging at my bottom lip, his hands tugging my hair, his cock unrelenting in stroking my G-spot. I'm straddling that exquisite line between pleasure and pain in the same way I straddle him; knowing that if I can just let go, it'll be amazing.

I'm on the cusp of coming almost before I realize it. Some things get better with age and that, at least for me, seems to be one of them. I press my mouth to his shoulder and grind against him, feeling wetness flowing from me and soaking us both. And then I'm there, right there, biting his shoulder harder than I should be to keep from screaming. I succeed—almost—and the squeak-moan that comes out of me would be funny if it wasn't a verbal testament for every single emotion I feel for this man.

He's whispering in my ear, a string of nonsensical obsceni-ties and encouragements, meant to drive me higher—but I'm already there, as high as I can be, looking down at him and wanting him to join me. My eyes are heavy-lidded with lust and I see him almost as a blur, intense blue eyes staring into mine, his mouth quirked into a smile that is part amusement at my arousal and all male satisfaction to be the one to cause it.

"Your turn, baby. I want you to come inside me," I whisper, sounding like a siren, a temptress, a vixen. I am all these things with him, for him. "Please."

It's the *please* that does it. I know this, of course. His orgasm was a foregone conclusion the minute we closed the bedroom door, but knowing I want it—want him—and am willing to ask or even beg for it, sets him off. He digs his fingers into my hips, anchoring me on him as he thrusts up harder and deeper than before. With him buried inside me, I feel his pulse and then release. His jaw is clenched, that vein throbbing in time with his cock, as a guttural moan rises up deep and primal, sending a shiver up my spine that makes me tighten around his cock.

We're both sweaty and panting as I collapse on top of him, feeling his heart pounding in his chest much as mine is pounding. That's what I needed—what I always seem to need and can never get enough of. I'm trailing kisses along his shoulder, still not able to get enough of him, always wanting more. I don't realize I'm crying until he shifts his weight and rolls me over on my side so he can look at me.

"You okay, babe?"

I laugh softly, rubbing the tears away. "I'm great. My body just turned on the waterworks—everywhere."

He doesn't laugh with me. "Are you sure? You'd tell me if something was wrong, right?"

It's my turn to reassure him, and I do. "Of course. You're the first one—the only one—I'd tell. I'm good. I'm great. I needed this, that's all. Needed it more than I realized."

"Me too," he confesses. "It's been a hell of a year."

"Hell of a decade."

He nods, staring at me still. It's as if we both are afraid to look away, afraid to break the spell. But that's silly. It's always there, between us, even when we're not together. We just need to find more of these times, whatever it takes.

His serious expression shifts to playful when his mouth quirks up into a smile. "Well, it's only nine-thirty, you know."

His smile is contagious. "Yeah? What were you thinking? Ice cream and an episode of *Game of Thrones*?"

His semi-hard cock suggests something else. "Maybe later," he says, rolling me onto my back and pressing the head of his cock against my still-sensitive clit. "We have to make the most of the alone time we get, right?"

Wrapping my legs around his waist and digging my fingers into his well-muscled ass, all I can do is nod. Yes, yes, yes.

ABOUT THE AUTHORS

LAILA BLAKE (lailablake.com) is a linguist, working as a translator and English teacher in Cologne, Germany. She has yet to find a genre to settle down with but most prominently enjoys writing romance and erotica. Her first novel, *By the Light of the Moon,* was released in April 2013.

VICTORIA BLISSE (victoriablisse.co.uk) is equally at home behind a laptop or cooker and loves to create stories and baked goods that make people happy. Passion, love and laughter fill her works, just as they fill her busy life.

The story goes that while on pregnancy bed rest, **LAUREN DANE's** (laurendane.com) husband bought her a secondhand laptop. She wrote her first book on it and never looked back. Today, Lauren is a *New York Times* and *USA Today* best-selling author of over fifty novels and novellas across several genres.

EMERALD's erotic fiction has been published in anthologies edited by Violet Blue, Rachel Kramer Bussel and Kristina Wright, among others. She is an advocate for reproductive freedom and sex-worker rights and blogs about both at thegreenlightdistrict.org. At age fifteen, she started wanting to dye her hair purple.

LUCY FELTHOUSE (lucyfelthouse.co.uk) writes erotica and erotic romance in a variety of subgenres and pairings, and has over seventy publications to her name, with many more in the pipeline. Anthology appearances include *Best Bondage Erotica 2012* and *2013*, and *Best Women's Erotica 2013*.

A naughty girl on a journey of self-discovery as an erotic writer, **TAMSIN FLOWERS** (tamsinflowers.com) is as keen to entertain her readers as she is to explore every aspect of female erotica. Hoping to touch you on your most erotic zones, she writes light-hearted stories that are sexy and fun.

JEANETTE GREY started out with degrees in physics and painting, which she dutifully applied to stunted careers in teaching, technical support, and advertising. When none of that panned out, she started writing. In her free time, Jeanette enjoys making pottery and playing board games. She lives in upstate New York.

A. M. HARTNETT (amhartnett.com) published her first erotic short in 2006. Since then, she has been featured in several anthologies, including Cleis's *Irresistible, Going Down, Sudden Sex* and *Best Erotic Romance 2013*. She has also written three novels as Annemarie Hartnett.

CRYSTAL JORDAN is originally from California, but has lived all over the United States. She currently serves as a librarian at a university in her home state and she writes paranormal, contemporary, futuristic and erotic romance. Her publishers have included Kensington Aphrodisia, Harlequin Spice Briefs, Ellora's Cave and Samhain Publishing.

ANNABETH LEONG (annabethleong.blogspot.com) knows a timing belt from a steering wheel, but just barely. She writes erotic romance for Ellora's Cave, Breathless Press, and others and has contributed to more than twenty anthologies, including *Best Bondage Erotica 2013* and *Passion: Erotic Romance for Women*.

NIKKI MAGENNIS (nikkimagennis.com) is an author, artist and poet. She has published two erotic novels and over thirty short stories—erotic, literary and romantic. She lives in Scotland with her family and is learning the art of stopping time.

KELLY MAHER's (kellymaher.com) published works include the story "Homecoming" in *Duty and Desire: Military Erotic Romance*. She currently lives in Washington, DC where she is working on a historical adventure romance and an urban fantasy series in addition to her erotic short stories.

CATHERINE PAULSSEN's (catherinepaulssen.com) stories have appeared in the 2012 and 2013 editions of *Best Lesbian Romance, Girl Fever* and *Duty and Desire* (all published by Cleis Press), in Silver Publishing's *Dreaming of a White Christmas* series and in anthologies by Ravenous Romance and Constable & Robinson.

Award-winning erotica writer **GISELLE RENARDE** is a queer Canadian, avid volunteer, contributor to more than one hundred short-story anthologies, and author of numerous electronic and print books, including *Anonymous*, *Nanny State* and *My Mistress' Thighs*. Ms. Renarde lives across from a park with two bilingual cats who sleep on her head.

D. R. SLATEN began writing at a very young age. She spent most of her childhood with stories running in her head side by side with real stories in her life. Raising children and practicing law sidetracked her from her stories. Now, her stories have revolted and found a way out.

ANJA VIKARMA is an author living in the boondocks of upstate New York. Most recently, she was published in the anthology *Stretched: Erotic Fiction that Fondles the Imagination* and her work can be found on GoodVibesBlog.com. In addition to writing, Anja teaches yoga and creative writing, plays in a rock band and is an amateur tap dancer.

ABOUT THE EDITOR

Described by The Romance Reader as a "force to be reckoned with," **KRISTINA WRIGHT** (kristinawright.com) is the editor of the best-selling *Fairy Tale Lust: Erotic Fantasies for Women*, as well as several other Cleis Press anthologies including *Dream Lover: Paranormal Tales of Erotic* Romance; *Steamlust: Steampunk Erotic Romance*; *Lustfully Ever After: Fairy Tale Erotic Romance*; *Duty and Desire: Military Erotic Romance* and the *Best Erotic Romance* series, as well as the author/editor of *Bedded Bliss: A Couple's Guide to Lust Ever After*. She is also the author of *Seduce Me Tonight* for HarperCollins Mischief. Her erotica and erotic romance fiction has appeared in over one hundred anthologies and her articles, interviews and book reviews have appeared in numerous publications, both print and online. She received the Golden Heart Award for Romantic Suspense from Romance Writers of America for her first novel *Dangerous Curves*. She holds degrees in English and humanities and has taught composition and world mythology at the college level. Originally from South Florida, Kristina is living happily ever after in Virginia with her husband Jay and their two little boys.

Happy Endings Forever And Ever

Dark Secret Love
A Story of Submission
By Alison Tyler

Inspired by her own BDSM exploits and private diaries, Alison Tyler draws on twenty-five years of penning sultry stories to create a scorchingly hot work of fiction, a memoir-inspired novel with reality at its core. A modern-day *Story of O*, a *9 1/2 Weeks*-style journey fueled by lust, longing and the search for true love.
ISBN 978-1-57344-956-4 $16.95

High-Octane Heroes
Erotic Romance for Women
Edited by Delilah Devlin

One glance and your heart will melt—these chiseled, brave men will ignite your fantasies with their courage and charisma. Award-winning romance writer Delilah Devlin has gathered stories of hunky, red-blooded guys who enter danger zones in the name of duty, honor, country and even love.
ISBN 978-1-57344-969-4 $15.95

Duty and Desire
Military Erotic Romance
Edited by Kristina Wright

The only thing stronger than the call of duty is the call of desire. *Duty and Desire* enlists a team of hot-blooded men and women from every branch of the military who serve their country and follow their hearts.
ISBN 978-1-57344-823-9 $15.95

Smokin' Hot Firemen
Erotic Romance Stories for Women
Edited by Delilah Devlin

Delilah delivers tales of these courageous men breaking down doors to steal readers' hearts! *Smokin' Hot Firemen* imagines the romantic possibilities of being held against a massively muscled chest by a man whose mission is to save lives and serve *every* need.
ISBN 978-1-57344-934-2 $15.95

Only You
Erotic Romance for Women
Edited by Rachel Kramer Bussel

Only You is full of tenderness, raw passion, love, longing and the many emotions that kindle true romance. The couples in *Only You* test the boundaries of their love to make their relationships stronger.
ISBN 978-1-57344-909-0 $15.95

Red Hot Erotic Romance

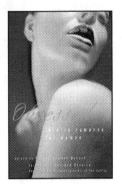

Obsessed
Erotic Romance for Women
Edited by Rachel Kramer Bussel

These stories sizzle with the kind of obsession that is fueled by our deepest desires, the ones that hold couples together, the ones that haunt us and don't let go. Whether just-blooming passions, rekindled sparks or reinvented relationships, these lovers put the object of their obsession first.
ISBN 978-1-57344-718-8 $14.95

Passion
Erotic Romance for Women
Edited by Rachel Kramer Bussel

Love and sex have always been intimately intertwined—and *Passion* shows just how delicious the possibilities are when they mingle in this sensual collection edited by award-winning author Rachel Kramer Bussel.
ISBN 978-1-57344-415-6 $14.95

Girls Who Bite
Lesbian Vampire Erotica
Edited by Delilah Devlin

Bestselling romance writer Delilah Devlin and her contributors add fresh girl-on-girl blood to the pantheon of the paranormal. The stories in *Girls Who Bite* are varied, unexpected, and soul-scorching.
ISBN 978-1-57344-715-7 $14.95

Irresistible
Erotic Romance for Couples
Edited by Rachel Kramer Bussel

This prolific editor has gathered the most popular fantasies and created a sizzling, no-holds-barred collection of explicit encounters in which couples turn their deepest desires into reality.
978-1-57344-762-1 $14.95

Heat Wave
Hot, Hot, Hot Erotica
Edited by Alison Tyler

What could be sexier or more seductive than bare, sun-warmed skin? Bestselling erotica author Alison Tyler gathers explicit stories of summer sex bursting with the sweet eroticism of swimsuits, sprinklers and ripe strawberries.
ISBN 978-1-57344-710-2 $15.95

Out of This World Romance

Steamlust
Steampunk Erotic Romance
Edited by Kristina Wright

Shiny brass and crushed velvet; mechanical inventions and romantic conventions; sexual fantasy and kinky fetish: this is a lush and fantastical world of women-centered stories and romantic scenarios, a first for steampunk fiction.
ISBN 978-1-57344-721-8 $14.95

The Sweetest Kiss
Ravishing Vampire Erotica
Edited by D. L. King

These sanguine tales give new meaning to the term "dead sexy" and feature beautiful bloodsuckers whose desires go far beyond blood.
ISBN 978-1-57344-371-5 $15.95

Dream Lover
Paranormal Tales of Erotic Romance
Edited by Kristina Wright

A potent potion of fun and sexy tales filled with male fairies and clairvoyant scientists, as well as darkly erotic tales of ghosts, shapeshifters and possession.
ISBN 978-1-57344-655-6 $14.95

Fairy Tale Lust
Erotic Fantasies for Women
Edited by Kristina Wright

Award-winning novelist and erotica writer Kristina Wright goes over the river and through the woods to find the sexiest fairy tales ever written.
ISBN 978-1-57344-397-5 $14.95

In Sleeping Beauty's Bed
Erotic Fairy Tales
By Mitzi Szereto

"Who can resist the erotic origins of fairy tales from Little Red to Rapunzel's long braid? Szereto knows her way around the mythic scholarship and the most outrageous sexual deviations in Pandora's Box."
—Susie Bright
ISBN 978-1-57344-367-8 $16.95

---

* Free book of equal or lesser value. Shipping and applicable sales tax extra.
Cleis Press • (800) 780-2279 • orders@cleispress.com
www.cleispress.com

Ordering is easy! Call us toll free or fax us to place your MC/VISA order.
You can also mail the order form below with payment to:
Cleis Press, 2246 Sixth St., Berkeley, CA 94710.

ORDER FORM

QTY	TITLE	PRICE
_____	_____	_____
_____	_____	_____
_____	_____	_____
_____	_____	_____
_____	_____	_____
_____	_____	_____
_____	_____	_____
_____	_____	_____

SUBTOTAL _____

SHIPPING _____

SALES TAX _____

TOTAL _____

Add $3.95 postage/handling for the first book ordered and $1.00 for each additional book. Outside North America, please contact us for shipping rates. California residents add 9% sales tax. Payment in U.S. dollars only.

★ **Free book of equal or lesser value. Shipping and applicable sales tax extra.**

Cleis Press • Phone: (800) 780-2279 • Fax: (510) 845-8001
orders@cleispress.com • www.cleispress.com
You'll find more great books on our website

Follow us on Twitter @cleispress • Friend/fan us on Facebook